CW00847485

LAYLA'S SCORE

A CRIME NOVEL

ANDY RAUSCH

For Jordan, Jaiden, Jalyn, and Josslyn, who were all Layla at one time or another.

Julian, you might have been a boy, but you're Layla too.

Inspired and influenced by:

Quentin Tarantino
Elmore Leonard
S. Craig Zahler
Joe R. Lansdale
Max Allan Collins
Shane Black
Richard Stark
Don Pendleton

NOTE

The character Orlando Williams previously appeared as the protagonist in the novel *The Suicide Game*. However, this should not be seen as a sequel, but rather a completely separate story.

I look at the helpless bundle in the crib and she looks up at me and I wonder what I would not do to protect her. I would lay down my life in a second. And truth be told, if push came to shove, I would lay down yours too.

HARLAN COBEN, *NO SECOND CHANCE*

Hell is never far away.

LORENZO CARCATERRA, *THE WOLF*

PROLOGUE

LEFTY COLLINS MADE *his way quietly through the mark's crib, his silenced Glock 23 in hand, ready to be used should the need arise. The mark's stereo was playing loudly, and music filled the place. It was Eric Clapton. As Lefty walked, he paid no mind to the lavish interior of the mark's home, a big mansion worth a couple million easy. Lefty had neither the time nor inclination to gawk at the man's possessions. Other people who'd grown up in the neighborhood Lefty had would have stopped and taken note of this assemblage of expensive crap, but not him. He was here to do a job. Beyond that, he didn't want to know a damned thing about this man. He didn't want to see the mark as an actual human being. Doing so would only make his job more difficult.*

He passed the stereo and turned slightly towards a hallway. He sensed the mark was somewhere down there, in the bowels of the mansion. Lefty moved slowly into the hallway, prepared to shoot at any moment. He came to the first room, which was filled with arcade-style cabinet video games from the 1980s. Lefty had enjoyed these games as a kid—he could see Galaga and Frogger there, just to name two—but he paid them no mind. He continued down the hall. He passed framed photographs of the mark posing with friends, family, and celebrities like Michael Jordan and Barack Obama, but he didn't look at them.

As he came to each bedroom, he looked in and found them empty. After passing several rooms, he came to one at the end of the hallway. The door was open just a bit, and there was light inside. Lefty could hear the shower running. He leaned his head in towards the door, listening for additional sounds, but heard only the shower. He slowly pushed the door open with the silencer of his Glock. As he did, waves of steam from the hot shower came cascading out. Lefty made his way towards the shower, which was along the wall at the back of the room. There was a shower curtain closed, and Lefty could see the figure of a man inside. Luckily the shower curtain was beige, so neither he nor the man inside the shower could get a good luck at the other.

He moved closer to the shower, his raised Glock a few inches from the curtain. This was when the man shut off the water. Lefty tensed up, and the man pulled the curtain back. Lefty saw a black man and a black woman standing there, naked, startled by his presence. Lefty recognized the man as his mark. Before anyone could move or say a word, Lefty squeezed the trigger. The first shot struck the man in the eye, and the second caught the woman in her left cheek. Their brains painted the white tile wall of the shower and they dropped into lifeless piles of skin and bones. Lefty was pretty sure they were dead, but he shot each of them once more to be sure.

He turned and made his way out of the bathroom. He was just turning into the hall when he heard a sound coming from inside one of the dark rooms he'd passed. It was the unmistakable sound of a small child crying for its mother.

The realization that came with this horrified the hitman. He made his way towards the sound, and entered the room he'd previously believed to be empty. There was a small child, probably about two, standing beside a Mickey Mouse toddler bed. It was dark, so Lefty used the gloved hand carrying the Glock to switch on the light. He looked at the little girl, unsure what to do next. The thought of shooting the child crossed his mind, sickening him.

The little girl stopped crying and looked up at him. She made a nonsensical baby noise that sounded gleeful, probably happy someone had come to save her from bedtime.

"What's your name, little girl?" asked Lefty.

The toddler had no idea what he was saying and stared at him blankly. Eric Clapton was singing "Layla" in the next room. And so it goes.

ONE

LOVE AND HAPPINESS

THEY WERE CLOSE TO ST. Louis, midway through the eleven-hour drive from Chicago to Tulsa, when Layla had to go potty. Lefty told the little girl, "Gimme a couple minutes, Tator Tot. I gotta find a spot for you to pee." As he went to work scanning the road for a suitable place, Layla blurted, *"You'd better hurry! I gotta go bad!"*

Lefty looked at her in the rear-view mirror. Her face was contorted and she was twisting uncomfortably. "How bad?"

"Real bad, Daddy."

"You need to tell me when you first feel it coming on," said Lefty. "You gotta give me time to find someplace to take you. You can't just wait until you're about to explode and then expect me to find a gas station in two seconds. There aren't any gas stations around here."

"But I didn't know I had to pee until just now," she said, her voice shrill and whiny, as urgent as he'd ever heard it.

Lefty's eyes continued to scan the road, occasionally glancing at the little girl in the back seat, writhing uncomfortably. Finally, after a couple minutes, he came to the conclusion that he had to do something immediately or the seven-year-old was going to have an accident. He pulled off onto a small county road. Seeing there weren't any businesses beyond the highway, he stopped the Caddy on the side of road, its frame leaning into the ditch.

Layla said again, "I gotta go pee, Daddy. I gotta go real bad."

Lefty unbuckled his seatbelt and made eye contact with her in the mirror. "I know, Tator Tot." He opened the door and climbed out, making his way back to Layla's door. He opened it and found Layla unbuckling her belt. He let her out, looking down the road to make sure there were no vehicles approaching.

The little girl looked around. "Where's the bathroom, Daddy?"

"There's no bathroom, Tator Tot."

She looked at him quizzically. "Then where should I potty?"

Lefty nodded toward the ditch. "Right here."

She looked at the ditch, confused and unsure. "I don't wanna pee *outside*."

"I understand that, kid, but if you don't pee now, you're gonna pee your pants. That's a no-no. Think how yucky it's gonna feel wearing cold pee pants. So—"

"So what?"

"You gotta pee outside."

She wasn't pleased about this development, but she took it in stride. Layla was smarter than the average seven-year-old and Lefty had found that most of the time he could simply explain things to her as though she were an adult. There were of course exceptions, but for the most part this was true.

She made her way down into the ditch. "How do I do it, Daddy? I never pottied outside before."

Lefty looked to the heavens, taking a slow breath. Showing a little girl how to pee outside without getting any on her clothes was not something he'd ever imagined he'd be doing. "Pull your pants down, to your socks," he said. To his surprise, without much resistance, Layla slid her tiny blue jeans down around her ankles. "You gotta pull down your panties, too," he said. *"Really?"* she asked. This made him chuckle. "Unless you wanna pee through your undies, then yeah, you gotta slide those down, too." Again the little girl accepted his word and slid her panties down, now standing there with her privates exposed to all of Missouri.

She looked at him. "Now what, Daddy?"

"You just gotta pee, right?" he asked. "No poop?"

"No poop."

"Okay," he said. "You gotta squat down and stick your butt out so when you pee you won't get any on your pants or your shoes."

"I don't sit on anything?" she asked, unsure. "I just pee with my bottom in the air?"

"That's how you do it."

"Why?"

Having no sufficient answer for this, Lefty replied, "That's just the way it's done. There's no reason why, that's just how it is."

"Okay," she agreed, starting to strain to make the urine flow.

As she did this, Lefty glanced down the road and saw a white car approaching. He squinted his eyes, trying to see it better. It came closer and he realized it was a cop.

"Shit," he said, unsure what the best course of action might be.

He looked at Layla. "It's starting to come out now," she said.

"I'm sure it is," he muttered. There was no way out. The cop was approaching, slowing as he did. Lefty could just imagine how this looked, a black man standing on the side of the road next to an expensive car, hovering over a little girl pissing in a ditch. And considering how close they were to Ferguson, where the cops had famously killed an unarmed black man named Michael Brown, Lefty wasn't overly excited about the prospect of being stopped here.

Maybe it would be a black cop, he reasoned. They weren't much better, Uncle Toms really, but that would dramatically decrease his chances of being gunned down in front of his little girl. The cop pulled up, and Lefty could see his face. He was as white as a paper plate blowing in a snow storm.

Here we go, he thought.

The cop was staring at Layla through the window of his cruiser.

Lefty looked down at her squatting there. "You about done, Tator Tot?"

"Almost done, Daddy."

The cop stopped and got out of the cruiser. Luckily he didn't have his hand anywhere near his pistol. As he walked around the car, the cop said, "Little girl had to go pee, huh?" There was a big smirk on his face.

"She did," Lefty said, nodding.

Layla heard the cop but was completely unfazed by his presence. She remained there, squatting, focused on the task at hand.

Lefty looked at the cop, trying to look as nice and smiley and white-people friendly as he could.

"I got three daughters of my own," said the cop. "I been down this road before."

There wasn't anything in the cop's voice that led Lefty to believe there was gonna be trouble. Not yet, anyway.

Lefty started to respond, but Layla spoke first. "I'm done, Daddy. What do I do now?"

Lefty looked at her, and then back at the cop, unsure what he should do.

"You got any napkins?" asked the cop.

Lefty hadn't even considered this. "Yeah," he said. "I'm pretty sure." He climbed into the car and opened the glove compartment, but couldn't find any napkins. He considered pulling out the Glock, but he didn't want to do any gangster shit in front of Layla. "Dammit," he said.

"Ain't got no napkins?" asked the cop.

"It doesn't look like it."

"What were you gonna use to let the little girl wipe with?"

"I hadn't really given it much thought," said Lefty. "We hadn't gotten that far. She had to go, so we stopped. This was our first go-around with this type of thing."

The cop went back to the cruiser. "I'm pretty sure I got some Dairy Queen napkins in the car. I'll go look."

Good lord, thought Lefty. *What have I gotten my black ass into?*

"What do I do now, Daddy?"

"Just a second," said Lefty. "The nice policeman is gonna get some napkins so you can wipe, just like you do when you sit on the toilet."

"Good," she said. "I was hoping I could wipe."

Lefty looked over at the cop, reemerging from the cruiser with a handful of brown napkins. He brought them

9

to Lefty, who then carried them to Layla. "Here you go, Tator Tot," he said. "Wipe with these."

She took the napkins. "What do I do with the napkin after I wipe my pee on it?"

Lefty didn't know. He looked at the cop, who was on the verge of real laughter. "Just throw it on the ground," said the cop. "Someone gets paid to pick up the trash around here. Leaving trash behind, that's job security for those fellas. I wouldn't recommend throwing out your trash all the time, but this once ain't gonna hurt nothin'." He looked at Lefty. "Who wants to carry around a napkin with piss on it, am I right?"

Lefty nodded, glancing over at Layla wiping.

"I'm done," she announced. "Now what?"

"Drop the napkin on the ground and pull up your pants."

Layla looked at him, a serious expression on her face. "I can't litter."

"What?" asked Lefty.

"I can't litter. Because it's wrong."

"Who says?"

"My teacher told us it destroys the environment."

The cop chuckled. "A napkin lying on top of the ground won't hurt the environment. It might irritate the person who's gotta pick it up, but that's about it. It really won't do too much of anything bad."

The little girl looked at him. "Are you sure?"

"Of course," said the cop. "I'm a policeman. Would I lie to you?"

"I don't know," said Layla.

Lefty looked at her. "Just throw the napkin on the ground, Layla. It'll be fine."

Layla didn't approve, but she finally dropped the pee-stained napkin in the ditch. Lefty looked back at the cop, whose demeanor was gradually shifting to one more business-like. "You the little girl's father?"

Lefty nodded.

The cop looked at Layla, now standing, pulling her pants up around her waist.

"Hey, little girl?" said the cop.

Layla looked at him innocently. "Yes?"

"What's your name?"

"My name's Layla. What's yours?"

The cop laughed and looked at Lefty, then back at Layla. "My name's Jim."

She smiled. "Hi, Jim."

"Hi, Layla," the cop said. "I gotta question for you. Is this man your daddy?"

Layla's face brightened. "Yep, he sure is. He's my daddy alright."

The cop looked at him, sizing him up. "He a pretty good daddy?"

She nodded. "He's the best daddy in the whole wide world."

The cop nodded. "Glad to hear that." He looked at Lefty. "Where you headed?"

"Tulsa."

"What's in Tulsa?"

Lefty wanted to be a smart ass and say, "Tulsa residents," but thought the better of it. Instead he said, "I haven't been in there in years. I thought it might be fun to take the little girl there. When I was a kid I used to spend summers there with my Auntie Mae. She used to take us to this big amusement park they had there, was open every day. I loved that place, and I think she's gonna love it, too."

"You know they got an amusement park up the road in

St. Louis?" asked the cop. "Six Flags. I used to take my kids there every summer."

"I've heard that," said Lefty. "But I ain't never been."

"It's pretty good. But it ain't cheap."

"Nothing is. Not anymore."

"You said a mouthful there," said the cop.

"The one in Tulsa is called Bell's Amusement Park. They got a big roller coaster there and me and my brother Marky used to ride on it all day long, over and over," said Lefty. "And there was this Mexican restaurant there my auntie used to take us to…"

The cop was confused. "There was a Mexican restaurant inside the amusement park?"

"No," said Lefty. "It was somewhere else in Tulsa. But it was good. It was called Casa Bonita. Auntie Mae used to take us there all the time to get enchiladas, and those were some good-assed enchiladas."

"Oh yeah?"

Lefty grinned. "Best enchiladas I ever had."

"I like tamales," said the cop. "So your auntie, she still live in Tulsa?"

"Nah, she's gone now, goin' on twenty years."

The cop nodded, understanding.

Lefty leveled his gaze at him. "Cancer."

"Cancer's a bitch," said the cop. "My old man died of cancer."

"I'm sorry to hear that."

"So was he. But you know what? He was a miserable old sonofabitch, so maybe it was karma. You believe in karma?"

"Not really."

The cop didn't even acknowledge Lefty's answer, he just kept on talking. "He didn't even know he had the cancer. He started feeling bad and then one day, out of the blue, he fell down and hurt himself. They took him in to get checked out. They ran all kinds of blood tests and we waited for days to get the results. When they finally came back, they said he had cancer. It had spread into his brain, lungs, and kidneys."

"No shit?" asked Lefty.

"And you know what?" The cop paused for effect. "My old man died the next day, I shit you not. The very next day. It all went South that quickly."

"That's horrible."

"I was at work, staked out in front of some meth dealer's house. My old man went into a coma, and they called and said he wasn't gonna wake up again."

"So you didn't get to say goodbye?"

"Well," the cop said, his eyes watering just a bit, "they put the phone up to his ear and let me talk to him. I don't know if he heard any of it. I suspect he didn't, but they said it was good for me to do it anyway. I couldn't even get through it without crying. I got embarrassed and hung up the damn phone before the nurse even got back on the line."

"I'm sorry, man," said Lefty, trying to figure out how he'd gotten into the curious predicament of consoling a white cop in the middle of nowhere.

"With all the money they spend on weapons to fight the sand niggers—" The cop caught himself. He looked up at Lefty, an awkward expression on his face, and then tried to pretend he'd never said it. "You'd think, with all the money they got for other things, they would figure out a cure for cancer."

Lefty nodded. "I suppose there's more money in it if they don't find a cure."

The cop started to say something else, but Layla interrupted. "When are we gonna go, Daddy?"

Lefty looked at the cop. "Are we good here?"

The cop nodded. "Yeah, I think we're good. But next time the little girl's gotta pee, try to find a bathroom."

"We will. What happened was, she waited until the last second, and there wasn't time. If I had waited, she woulda peed in the car."

The cop nodded. "Trust me, I've been there. Just do your best, friend."

He climbed back into his cruiser and drove away, giving a small wave as he did.

THEY HAD JUST PASSED ST. Louis when Lefty decided to converse with Layla. For the past couple hours she'd been playing some kind of robot game on her tablet. The only way he'd been able to get her away from the thing for any small amount of time was to ask her for details about the game. She took a break to tell him about it, but damned if he didn't understand a single word of what she'd said. After that, once she'd finished describing the game, she'd gone right back to playing it, seemingly transported to somewhere far, far away.

To keep himself busy, Lefty listened to Parliament on the stereo. He played the greatest hits album all the way from "Up for the Down Stroke" to "Black Hole (Theme)" without Layla saying a single word. Finally he said, "Hey, Tator Tot." He looked at her in the rear-view mirror. Layla said, "What?," without even looking up from her game.

"We're gonna take a break from the tablet."

That got her attention. She looked up, a startled look on her face. *"Really?"* she asked, sounding pained.

Lefty nodded. "Really, Tator Tot."

"But why?"

"Just turn it off," he said. "We're gonna talk for a little bit. God forbid you actually have to talk to your daddy some."

She slumped unhappily. "But I was just getting to the good part." This meant nothing, as Lefty had learned from previous conversations that she was always just getting to the good part; seemingly every part of her game was the good part and she didn't like being interrupted.

"Turn it off, baby."

Layla was displeased, but being the good girl she was, she did as she was instructed.

She looked at him up in the mirror. "What now, Daddy?"

"I wanna talk to you," he said. "That okay with you?"

"What do you wanna talk about?"

"We can talk about anything."

The broadness of his reply seemed to pique her interest. "*Anything?*"

"Sure," he said. "What do you wanna talk about?"

"Can we talk about NASA?"

He looked at her, blinking as he did. "*NASA?* That's what you wanna talk about?"

"I like NASA."

"Okay," said Lefty. "NASA's good."

"Did you know I was two-years-old when Neil Armstrong died?"

"Hmm. Does that make you sad?"

"Yes," she said matter-of-factly. "Now I'll never get to meet him."

"What would you have done if you had gotten to meet him?"

"I'd have told him he was my hero," she said. "Someday I'm gonna be an astronaut just like Neil Armstrong. Is that okay? Do you think I would be a good astronaut?"

Lefty nodded. "Sure, I don't see why not. But I wouldn't want you to get hurt."

"I wouldn't get hurt, Daddy. I promise."

"Pinky promise?"

Layla said solemnly, "Pinky promise."

"Well, then I guess it's okay."

"You know what else I'm gonna be when I grow up?"

He humored her. "What are you gonna do, Tator Tot?"

"I'm gonna be a police officer, like Jim back there," she said. Lefty's heart sank, and he could feel his features twisting into a disapproving expression. "You're gonna be what?"

"I wanna be a cop," she said proudly.

"Why do you wanna be a cop?"

She looked at him, beaming. "I wanna help people."

"Is that what you think cops do?" he asked. "Help people?"

"Of course, silly. They help everyone."

"I don't know," he said. "It seems to me like there are other jobs you could be that might be better."

She frowned. "Better than being a cop?"

"Sure," he said.

"What's wrong with being a cop?"

"Well," he began weakly, "some cops are good, and some cops are bad."

"There are bad cops?" she asked, amazed by the thought. "I thought all cops were good. I thought they help people."

"Sometimes," said Lefty. "But some cops are mean. Some of them don't like black people."

Her expression was one of genuine interest. "I'm a black person, right Daddy?"

"Yes, Tator Tot. We're both black."

She looked at her arm, studying it. "Actually, I think I look more brown than black."

Lefty grinned. "That's true. We're both more brown than we are black, but that's what they call us—black."

"Who calls us that?"

He thought about it for a moment. "Society."

"What's society?"

Lefty recognized this was a rabbit hole he might never get out of, so he gave her a simple explanation. "Everyone. Society means everyone."

"Oh," she said, taking it in. "And cops don't like black people?"

"*Some* cops don't like black people. Not all of them."

"Daddy, why don't they like us?"

Lefty turned it over in his head for a moment before answering. That was a good question. "I don't know," he said. "I guess you'd have to ask them." He looked at her contemplating this and added, "We probably shouldn't really ask a cop about that."

"We shouldn't?"

"Probably not."

"Why's that, Daddy?"

"Well, if it's one of the cops who don't like black people, we wouldn't wanna make them mad. They might hurt us."

She looked up at him, her eyes big now. *"Hurt us?"*

"Yeah, baby," he said. "Sometimes cops hurt black people."

"How?"

"There's all kinds of ways. Sometimes they beat black

17

people up with those hard wooden sticks they have, and other times they just shoot them."

"*Shoot them?*" she asked, horrified. "With guns?"

It was horrific, to be sure. "Sometimes."

"Well, I don't wanna hurt anyone," she said. "I wanna be one of the nice cops."

Lefty nodded. She was only seven, so the chances of her actually mapping out her future right at this moment were pretty slim. So he let it go. She thought for a moment and then said, "You know what else I'm gonna be?"

"You're gonna have more jobs?"

"Yeah," she said. "I'm gonna have lots of jobs."

"How are you gonna work all those jobs at the same time?"

"Not at the same time, silly," she said. "I'll work them at different times. When I get done with one job I'll go to the next."

Lefty grinned. "That's how it works?"

"Of course."

"So what other jobs are you gonna have?"

She was excited now. "I'm gonna be a pizza chef."

"A pizza chef?"

"Yeah," she said. "I'm gonna make pizzas and I'm gonna have my own restaurant where I make them. And do you know how much they're gonna cost?"

"Two dollars?" he asked, kidding her.

"My pizzas are gonna be free, Daddy."

He grinned. "Free pizzas, huh?"

"That way everyone can have some," said Layla. "But they won't all be free."

"They won't?"

"Nope. Some pizzas will cost more."

"Why's that?"

"Because they're the ones made with the special ingredient."

"There's a special ingredient?"

"Yep," she said, feeling proud of herself.

"What's the special ingredient?"

Layla looked up at him, barely able to control her enthusiasm. "Love."

Lefty chuckled. "You got it all figured out."

"Yep."

They drove for about a mile in silence before Layla asked, "Can we listen to some music, Daddy?"

"More Parliament?"

"I don't like Parliament very much," said Layla.

"Then what kind of music do you wanna hear?"

She didn't hesitate, answering right away. "I wanna hear Al Green."

"You wanna listen to Al Green?"

"I wanna hear 'Love and Happiness.' That's a good song, isn't it, Daddy?"

"It sure is, Tator Tot." He smiled proudly with the knowledge that he was raising the girl right. The fact that Layla requested Al Green on her own was a good sign. He picked up the case from the floor and opened it, removing the CD. He slid it into the stereo and a moment later "Tired of Being Alone" came to life, filling the car. "Love and Happiness,'" she reminded him. He preferred "Tired of Being Alone," but skipped to track five per her request. The song began, and she sang along verbatim, stopping only to ask, "I sound as good as Al Green, don't I? Our voices really go together."

Lefty agreed with the assessment, and they continued driving.

· · ·

LEFTY STOPPED the Caddy at a McDonalds in Springfield, and the two went inside for lunch. "Daddy," Layla said, "can I have a Happy Meal?"

Knowing full well the whole Happy Meal deal was a scam, Lefty frequently said no to this request. Today he was feeling good, perhaps inspired by the positivity of Al Green or maybe just feeling good about the trip, so he allowed Layla to get the Happy Meal. His positive response caused her to celebrate, and she was literally jumping up and down with excitement. "Chicken nuggets, Daddy," she said. "With yogurt."

Of course he already knew all of this as Layla always requested the same thing, but he said nothing. When she didn't specifically point out that she wanted Hi-C to drink, he asked her if that's what she wanted, knowing full well it would be. And, of course, it was. He went to the counter and ordered the food. He then sat down with Layla, waiting less than two minutes for the food to be delivered to them.

Lefty made quick work of his two cheeseburgers, eating them in the same peculiar manner he always had, which was to lay out seven or eight French fries on top of the patties and under the bun, then dipping the sandwich in barbecue sauce. Layla, per usual, ate her nuggets very slowly—Lefty would have sworn she was the slowest eater on the planet—without dipping sauce of any kind.

"How far is it to Tulsa?" she asked.

"We're close now," he replied. "Only a couple more hours and we'll be there."

Layla nodded and went about eating her chicken nuggets, occasionally stopping for a sip of her Hi-C.

When they were finished, she asked, "Now what?"

"I figure we'll take a break for a bit. How does that sound?"

"That sounds good," said Layla. "Can we go to the park?"

"I don't know where the park is here."

She made a disappointed face, playing him like a fiddle. "Please, Daddy." As was most often the case, she succeeded in playing to his desire to please her and he said sure. They drove a block down the street to the Get-It-Quick gas station, where Lefty asked for directions to the nearest park. He was directed to a place called Jordan Valley Park, which was only a few minutes away. They went to the park and Lefty sat on a picnic table and watched Layla swing and play.

Finally, after a half hour had passed, he called her over. She sat down beside him and the two of them read a chapter from Stephen King's *Pet Sematary*, which they had been reading for the past week. Today they were reading about a zombie named "Paxcow" who had returned to pay a visit to the book's protagonist, Louis Creed. Once Lefty and Layla finished the chapter, he closed the book. "That's it for today, Tator Tot."

"That was scary," she said solemnly. "Don't you think so, Daddy? Wasn't that scary?"

"Sure, it's scary," he conceded. "That's why we read it—to get scared."

"Really?" She considered this for a moment. *"Why?"*

"Why what?"

"Why would we wanna get scared? Isn't that silly?"

Lefty grinned. "No, it's fun being scared. Don't you think?"

"I guess." She nodded and accepted his assertion unquestioningly.

He looked at her. "Wanna go shoot?"

Her eyes got big and her face lit up. *"Really? I get to shoot?"*

"Sure."

"The Glock 23, Daddy?"

As always, he sought to please her. "Of course," he said. "The Glock 23."

He then drove out of town onto the highway in search of an out-of-the-way road they might take to get to a secluded area where they could shoot. It took a couple of bad turns resulting in subpar locations, but finally, on the third try, Lefty found a suitable road that was off-the-beaten-path. After driving a ways away from the highway, he then made another turn, now completely out in the country, ensuring they would be smack dab in the middle of nowhere.

Once he was satisfied with the location, Lefty stopped the car. They climbed out and he retrieved some empty Coke cans and the previous night's empty Jack Daniels bottle from the trunk. He sat them on wooden fence posts, and then returned to the gravel road.

"Can I hold the Glock, Daddy?" asked Layla.

"In a minute," he said. "Daddy's gonna shoot first."

He raised the pistol, leveling it, and fired on the whiskey bottle, shattering it.

"Now my turn!"

Lefty walked around behind her, put his arms around hers, and the two of them reached out towards the empty Coke can. Even though he was behind her and couldn't see it, he knew, knowing this child as he did, that Layla was smiling big from ear to ear.

"Breathe in and out, slowly," he said. "Okay...breathe out. Slowly." She did as he instructed. "Now this time," he said, "we're gonna squeeze the trigger when we get to the end of that breath, okay?"

"Okay, Daddy."

The little girl calmly did what she'd been told to do, squeezing the trigger when she exhaled. The gun fired, making only a zip sound as it was muffled by a silencer. The shot went right, missing the can.

Layla slumped, disappointed. Lefty knew she was about to cry, so he cut her off, comforting her before the tears could come. "It's okay, Tator Tot," he said. "Everybody misses sometimes."

She twisted her head around to look at him. "Even you, Daddy?"

"Even me," he said, lying. "And you're still just learning. You're gonna get better every day."

"I will?"

"You absolutely will," he said. "You wanna try again?"

The little girl became animated once more, nodding excitedly. "Yes, please."

He stood behind her again, putting his arms over hers, and the two of them aimed the pistol, training it on the can. "Breathe in slowly," he said, then telling her, "now breathe out." When she reached the end of her exhalation, they squeezed the trigger again, this time hitting the can, which shot back into the high grass behind the post.

Layla got excited. "I hit it, Daddy! I hit the can!"

He took the pistol back from her, saying, "You did good, Tator Tot. You did real good."

TWO
TULSA CITY LIMITS

IT WAS JUST after five when they arrived in Tulsa. They were driving on Memorial when Lefty saw a Popeyes restaurant. Chicken sounded good and he was hungry. He pulled into the parking lot. Layla looked up from her tablet, curious about what was happening. "Why are we here, Daddy?"

"We're gonna get supper," said Lefty. "You want some chicken?"

"I thought we were gonna go to Casa Bonita."

"We just got here, and it's getting late. Why don't we save that for tomorrow? That'll give us something to look forward to."

Layla looked up at him. "I thought you were gonna meet that man tomorrow."

"I am," Lefty said. "But you and I are gonna have fun first."

"A daddy and daughter day?"

"You bet your butt."

This made Layla laugh. She was still at an age where she could be made to laugh by the mere mention of things like butts and farts. Lefty had always joked about wanting a job as a comedian for small children. "That shit would be the easiest job ever," he had said. After all, all the comedian would need to do was mention poop a few times, and the kids would laugh their asses off.

Lefty climbed out of the Caddy and opened Layla's door, letting her out. "Can I take my tablet inside?" she asked.

"Nope."

"Why not?"

"Because we're having dinner together," said Lefty. "You and I are gonna have a conversation, like civilized people do."

Layla tried to argue. "I can still talk while I play my game."

"Leave it in the car," he said firmly. She didn't want to do it, but she did. She closed the door and they walked inside the restaurant. Lefty was standing in line, eyeing the menu overhead.

"Can I have a kid's meal?" asked Layla.

"Not today, Tator Tot."

"Why?"

"It costs too much. We don't need to spend all our money."

"Can't you go to the bank and use your card to get some more money?"

"I could, but I'm not going to. Now look at the menu and figure out what you want to eat."

Layla stood there, biting her bottom lip and staring at the menu. "I want the fish and popcorn shrimp," she said. She considered this for a moment and asked, "What's popcorn shrimp, Daddy?"

25

"It's a kind of shrimp where you can eat the whole thing."

"Even the tails?"

Lefty nodded. "Even the tails."

"But it has popcorn in it?"

"No, Tator Tot. That's just what it's called, popcorn shrimp. It doesn't really have popcorn in it."

Layla frowned. "They shouldn't call it that then."

"Why don't you get some chicken? This is a chicken place after all."

"Then why do they sell fish?"

She had him there.

"Why don't you just go get us a table?" he asked.

"You'll get my food?"

"I'll get you chicken," he said. Layla frowned, but said nothing, walking into the dining area to secure a table. Lefty waited his turn. When he finally reached the front counter, he ordered spicy chicken tenders and a large order of beans and rice for himself. He thought about getting chicken for the girl, but relented and ordered the fish and popcorn shrimp. As much as he hated to admit it, even to himself, Layla had him wrapped around her finger.

While he waited on the food to be prepared, Lefty filled their cups with water and carried them to the table. He then went back and retrieved the tray of food. Once they were both sitting at the table, looking at their food, he said, "I got you the fish and shrimp like you wanted. Is there anything you'd like to say?"

"Thank you, Daddy."

She took a drink, then held the cup up and stared at it. "My Sprite tastes funny."

Lefty chuckled. "That's because it's water."

26

She stared at it for another moment before shrugging and taking another drink.

"What are we gonna do after this?" she asked.

"We can either go and get a motel room, or we can go to a movie first."

"I like motels."

"Is that what you wanna do? You wanna get a motel?"

"Not yet. I wanna go to a movie. What movies are there?"

"I don't know," said Lefty. "I haven't looked. I figure we'll just go there and see what's coming on. Then we'll just go see whatever they got."

They finished their meal. On the way out Lefty asked a random customer if he knew how to get to a movie theater. The man gave him directions, Lefty thanked him, and they were on their way.

Lefty found the theater easily. When they went inside, he scanned the options. It was a second-run theater. Lefty and Layla went to the movies at least once a week, so they had already seen most of them. One of the movies was a re-release of an old John Wayne movie called *The Searchers*. Lefty had seen it a few times, but Layla had not. He wasn't entirely sure she would like it, as she was still at an age where such things couldn't be easily predicted. It really could go either way.

Lefty approached the cashier. "One adult and one child for *The Searchers*." He paid for the tickets, got his change, and they went to the snack bar for refreshments. Layla asked, "What is this movie, Daddy?" He explained to her that it was a cowboy movie. She had only seen a handful of westerns, but she knew what they were. "Is it like *Unforgiven*?" To this he replied, "Yeah, kind of." He bought a box

27

of Milk Duds for himself and some Mike and Ikes for Layla, with a couple of Sprites to wash it all down.

When they entered the theater, the movie was already playing. Layla wanted to talk, but Lefty quieted her down. The theater was nearly empty. They sat in the rear, right in the middle. Layla occasionally asked questions regarding the events taking place on screen, but she was well-behaved. She fidgeted a little, which was to be expected for a child her age, and she lay her head on his shoulder about two-thirds of the way through. But she stayed awake and watched the movie in its entirety.

As they were walking out of the theater, Layla asked, "Debbie was a kid when she got kidnapped by those Indians, wasn't she?"

"She was," he agreed. "She was eight."

"And I'm seven," she said proudly.

"She was a year older than you."

She contemplated this. "Ethan looked for Debbie for a really long time," she said. "How long do you think he looked?"

"Several years."

"*Years?*" Layla bit her lip. "Daddy?"

"Yes, Tator Tot?"

"Can I ask you something?"

"Ask me anything."

"If Indians kidnapped me, would you look for me for years?"

"No."

She stopped and stared at him in disbelief, visibly upset. "*You wouldn't?*"

"I wouldn't need to," he said. "I'd find you right away and bring you back home. You wouldn't have to wait that long."

Layla brightened. "Daddy?"

"Yes, Tator Tot?"

"If someone kidnapped me, would you kill them like he did to that Indian?"

Lefty looked at her, serious now. "Of course I'd kill them, dead as disco."

Layla smiled. "I know you would." A moment later she said, "Daddy?"

"Yes, Layla?"

"What's disco?"

ONCE THEY WERE BACK in the Caddy, Lefty drove around for a few minutes searching for a place to stay. "What's the name of the motel we're gonna stay at?" asked Layla. Lefty told her he didn't know yet. Finally Lefty spotted a Motel Six. They pulled into the parking lot, got out, and checked in. As they carried their bags up to their second-floor room, Layla asked, "Can we go swimming, Daddy?"

"Not tonight," said Lefty. "It's too late."

"Are you sure?"

"They close the pool at night."

"But I wanna go."

Lefty considered this. He knew he was a pushover and was well aware that he should say no more frequently, but he relented. "When we get inside, you go in the bathroom and put on your swim suit."

Ten minutes later they were both wearing swim suits and standing at the front desk. "The little girl wants to go swimming," said Lefty. "Is there anything we can do about that?"

The Pakistani clerk smiled. "No problem. Go on in and swim. It's fine."

Lefty thanked him. The poor bastard had no idea he'd just missed out on a payoff. Lefty had been prepared to offer him as much as fifty bucks to let them swim. They ended up swimming for a half an hour before returning to their room, where Lefty watched *Taxi Driver* and Layla fell asleep.

THE NEXT MORNING they dined on complimentary breakfast consisting of cereal and rock-hard bagels before checking out at eleven. They both climbed into the Caddy, strapping on their seatbelts.

"What now, Daddy?"

"We're gonna go to Casa Bonita."

"Yay!" said Layla happily.

Lefty saw that the gas was low, beneath the quarter mark, so he turned the car into a QuikTrip on Mingo. He pulled up next to the pump and stopped. He looked back at Layla, staring down at a zombie game on her tablet, a zombie herself. "I'll be right back," he said. Layla continued staring at the game, unmoved. *"Layla!"* he snapped. She looked up, a little bit dazed and slightly irritated. "What, Daddy?"

"I'll be right back," said Lefty. "I'm gonna get gas."

"Okay," she said, her eyes back on the game.

Lefty shook his head as he climbed out. He reached into his pocket and pulled out his wallet, opening it and removing a credit card. He turned to the car and opened the fuel door. He turned back and swiped his card at the pump. He waited a moment and the screen inquired if he wanted a receipt. He pressed the button that said "no." It didn't register the first time, so he pressed it harder. This time it took. Lefty grabbed the handle of the nozzle and inserted the thing into the tank, pumping the gas.

As he stood there waiting for the tank to fill, he looked over at a hot little blonde chick, maybe 20, 22, getting gas at the next pump. She was bent over a bit, the cheeks of her shapely bottom bursting out from her tiny shorts. Lefty had an impure thought or two about both the girl and her bottom. He watched as she finished pumping her gas and then climbed back into her little red Suburu. Finally the lock on Lefty's nozzle clicked off, signifying that the tank was full. He removed the nozzle and repositioned it back in its holster.

He opened the car door and leaned in. "I'm gonna go to the bathroom." He could have been speaking to a wall, as its effect would have been exactly the same. Layla was lost in her own world, fighting computer zombies, completely oblivious to her surroundings. "Tator Tot," he said. She still didn't look up. *Fuck it*, he thought, closing the door. He walked around the vehicle and headed inside the QuikTrip. The bathroom was empty and he got in and used it quickly. When he was finished, he headed back towards the car.

Just as he was walking out of the QuikTrip, he saw his Caddy pulling away. He immediately broke into a sprint, to no avail. Still running, he watched the car pull out into the busy street. He kept running, jumping out into traffic in front of a guy in a gray van. The van jerked to a stop and the man honked angrily. Before he could take his hand away from the horn, Lefty was on him. He flung the door back, snatched the man, and pulled him out onto the street, dropping him. Lefty climbed into the van and stomped on the gas. The van lurched forward, leaving its owner lying behind. There was traffic, so Lefty had to swerve back and forth to progress towards the Caddy, way up ahead. As he approached an intersection, the traffic light turned yellow. *"Christ!"* he yelled. The light was red when he zipped through it, nearly being hit by a couple of cars on his right.

Lefty could see the Caddy, still quite a ways ahead. There were slow moving cars in front of him and he had no way to maneuver past them.

"Come on!" he yelled. As he approached another intersection, he could see the Caddy turning right. The lights were changing as he approached, and he was stuck in the left lane, unable to move towards the right one. He flipped on his turn signal, deciding he would sit there until he could get over into the right lane to turn and follow the carjacker. He considered jumping out, but knew that would be futile. Finally, after what felt like an eternity, the light changed. A couple cars passed by in the right lane before Lefty was able to swerve over, striking the front end of a pickup as he did. The pickup careened over the curb, and Lefty made a hard right, following the same route the Caddy had taken. But now the road ahead was empty, and the Caddy was nowhere to be seen.

"Motherfucker," he muttered, scanning the sides of the road, but not slowing down. As he rounded a curve, he spotted his car. It was way up ahead now, only one car between them. Lefty stomped the gas pedal to the floor, and the van shot forward. He continued gaining speed, coming up quickly on the vehicle between them. As he approached it, he swerved across the center line, into oncoming traffic, nearly being hit. He managed to get back into his lane, now just ahead of the vehicle he'd swerved around.

The Caddy was still quite a ways ahead, but he was closing in. He kept the gas pedal pressed all the way down to the floor, scenery zipping past him. He was closing in on the fucker, getting closer and closer. The Caddy was going somewhere around the speed limit, allowing Lefty to catch him rather quickly. Now the vehicle was right in front of him. Lefty continued accelerating, bumping the back of the Caddy with the front bumper of the van. The Caddy swerved from the impact, but the driver quickly regained control. Lefty pushed up on him again, tapping the Caddy a second time.

Lefty hoped Layla was okay. He had doubts the carjacker had hurt her. He wouldn't have had time since she was in the backseat and he was driving. The Caddy pulled off into the entrance of a fancy housing addition, and, to Lefty's surprise, it slowed. Before it could even come all the way to a stop, Lefty was out of the van, moving towards it. The driver's door opened and a skinny, dirty-looking methed-out white dude started to climb out. Before he could even fully stand, Lefty was on him, smashing him in the jaw with a hard right. The man tumbled back against the car, and Lefty grabbed a handful of his scraggly black hair and smashed his face down hard against the roof of the car. As the bloodied man slid down towards the pavement, Lefty caught him and kneed him hard in the crotch. The guy fell over, crumpling to the ground. Lefty stuck his head into the car, looking back at Layla sitting there. She looked shocked and had tears in her eyes, but she was alright.

"*Daddy!*" she screamed.

"Hi, Tator Tot," he said, breathing hard. "You stay here for a just minute. Daddy will be right back." He pulled the keys out of the ignition. With the keys in hand, he grabbed the fallen carjacker and dragged him on the pavement, back towards the rear of the Caddy. He pulled him around in front of the trunk. A car drove past, but all of this was obscured by the parked van. The guy didn't move. Lefty opened the trunk. He reached in and grabbed his Glock and the accompanying silencer. He screwed the silencer onto the pistol.

He stood over the man, still unconscious. "You fucked up, man," he said. "You fucked up real bad. Nobody hurts my little girl." He kicked him hard in the ribs, but the guy still didn't move. Lefty raised the pistol, training it on the man. "Nobody," he repeated, squeezing the trigger twice in quick succession. He tossed the Glock into the trunk and closed it. He walked around and got back in the car.

"I'm so happy to see you," said Layla excitedly. "I didn't think I'd ever see you again. You were right, Daddy. You rescued me from the bad man. You did what you said you'd do and you saved me." Lefty expected her to ask if he'd killed the man the way John Wayne had killed Scar, but the thought thankfully eluded her.

"Of course I saved you, Tator Tot," he said, backing the car up slowly. When the tires came to the man's body, the car climbed up over it, crushing bones as it did.

Layla's eyes were big. "What was that? Did we hit something?"

"We hit a rat."

"That musta been a big rat."

"Yeah," he said. "A great big rat. But we're okay now. Everything's good now, Tator Tot."

A moment passed and Layla had already moved on completely, the bad man who'd tried to steal both her and the car no longer a blip on her radar. "Are we going to Casa Bonita now?"

Lefty grinned at her. "Sure. It's time to go to Casa Bonita."

Lefty had looked up the address of the restaurant on the Internet, so he knew it was on Sheridan. When he came to Sheridan, he turned onto it. He wasn't a hundred percent sure exactly where the place was, so he drove slowly, looking around. Finally he saw the familiar building from his childhood. He turned into the parking lot. He couldn't see a sign, so he wasn't completely sure this was it. He drove up close to the building and saw that it was indeed the building he remembered. Unfortunately, it was no longer Casa Bonita. It was now a nightclub called Caves.

"Well, shit," he muttered. Layla didn't hear him as she was too busy fighting zombies. "Hey, kid." She looked up.

"What?"

"I'm afraid I got bad news."

Layla frowned. "Are they closed today?"

"Yeah, sort of," he said. "They're closed today. But the thing is, they're closed every day."

Layla didn't understand. "What do you mean?"

"They went out of business," he said. "Casa Bonita is gone."

"So we can't eat enchiladas?" she asked, a heavy sadness in her voice.

"Maybe we can get something else."

Layla asked, "Like what?"

"Anything you want, Tator Tot."

Layla thought about it for a moment. Then she said, "How about McDonalds?"

"Seriously?" he asked, wondering why kids always wanted McDonalds.

"Yeah."

"Baby," he said, "we can have McDonalds anytime back home. We're in a new city. Why don't we try something different?"

"But I want a Happy Meal."

"We're gonna try something different."

Layla did not attempt to hide her displeasure, but she didn't argue.

He tried to redirect her by saying, "After we eat we'll go to the amusement park. Won't that be fun?"

She brightened, sitting up. "I can't wait."

"Neither can I. But first we gotta find something to eat."

They wound up eating chili dogs at a place called Coney I-Lander. The place served chili dogs with mustard on them. Lefty had never eaten them with mustard, and was surprised to discover that he liked it. Per the usual, Layla ate very little, prompting Lefty to call her a "little bird."

When they were leaving, Lefty asked the guy behind the counter how to get to Bell's.

"Bell's Amusement Park?"

"Yeah, that's the one."

"That place has been closed for a decade."

"You're shitting me," said Lefty.

"I shit you not," said the man.

Lefty looked over at Layla, who was on the verge of tears. He hunkered down and put his arm around her. "It's okay, Layla," he consoled. "We'll find something else."

"But I wanted to ride the roller coaster."

"I know," he said. "So did I."

Layla soon regained her composure, using a power that is uniquely that of a seven-year-old, and was suddenly in good spirits again. "So now what?"

"You wanna go to the mall?"

"I guess," said Layla. "Malls are kinda boring."

Lefty had to agree. He'd enjoyed them when he was a kid, but since then all the stores he'd liked to go to had closed. There were no more music stores, video stores, or bookstores. The arrival of the Internet had stomped the hell out of those things, leaving them as dead as the guy who'd tried to steal Lefty's Caddy.

They wound up going to a place called Woodland Hills Mall. They were surprised to find a working carousel inside. For a quarter a ride people could take a whirl on the thing. Lefty and Layla rode several times. She was really picky, selecting a different horse for each ride. There was a bench on the carousel, so Lefty just sat there, watching the little girl.

There was a movie theater in the mall, so they wound up going to the movies again. This time they watched an action-comedy with Jackie Chan that had poor action and wasn't funny. Lefty hated it, but Layla loved it. When they were leaving the theater afterwards, she punched and kicked the air, pretending to be Jackie Chan.

Unsure what they should do next, Lefty looked up popular tourist attractions on his cell phone. After that, they went to an art museum called the Philbrook. As they walked around, admiring the paintings, Layla asked questions and explained things. "This is a Kandinsky," she explained, pointing at a painting.

Layla's intelligence never ceased to impress Lefty. "What do you know about Kandinsky?" he asked. He'd been the one who'd shown her the art book, but he'd already forgotten most of it. But not her. Layla rarely forgot anything. Her memory was nothing short of amazing.

"Vasily Kandinsky," said Layla. "He was born in Moxcow."

"Moscow," Lefty corrected.

"Moscow. He was an abstract painter. He had something called the Blue Rider Period, but I don't know what that means." She looked up at him. "What does that mean, Daddy?"

Lefty hated revealing the things he didn't know. He wanted to be her hero and he wanted to seem smart all the time. He didn't like to show her his ignorance. "Well, periods are different times in an artist's career, where all their paintings have a similar style. I don't know what the Blue Rider Period was specifically, but that's basically what it was—a time when all his paintings looked the same."

"Do you think this one's from the Blue Rider Period?"

Lefty shrugged. "I have no idea, kid."

When they were outside the museum and back in the car, Layla asked, "What do we do now, Daddy?"

The time had come. "Daddy needs to talk to a man about some business."

"What kind of business?"

"Grown-up stuff."

Layla accepted this and pressed no further.

AFTER USING the GPS on his phone to locate the residence, located on a street called East 24th Place, Lefty parked along the curb.

"Is this where he lives?" asked Layla.

"I think so."

The house was a modest little thing, the kind of place that was perfect for a single elderly man. It was neither too big nor too small. It was a well-kept, cozy-looking little blue house with a white one-car garage. Lefty sat there, listening to the Commodores sing "Easy" on the stereo. Once he got up his courage, he told Layla, "Stay here a minute. I'll be right back."

Layla looked up. "What if a mean man comes and takes me again?"

"It'll be fine," said Lefty. "The odds of that happening

again are slim. And I'll be right there on the porch. I'll talk to him, and then I'll come and get you."

"You'll come right back?"

"I promise."

"Pinky promise?"

"Pinky promise," said Lefty. He climbed out of the Caddy and walked up to the house.

"Here goes nothing," he said, knocking on the door. It took a minute, but a grizzled man of about seventy finally answered. He had the same irritable disposition a lot of old men had. "Yeah?" he asked in a gruff voice.

"Are you Brooks Barker?"

The man's eyes narrowed. "Who wants to know?"

"My name's Lefty. Spook Collins was my dad."

The old man looked at him, sizing him up. "Spook Collins was your old man?"

"He was."

"Well, hell," Brooks said. "Why didn't you say so? Come on in." He looked out at the Caddy. "Who you got out there with you?"

"That's my little girl, Layla. Can she come in?"

Brooks said, "Well, she can't stay out in the car all day. Bring her in. I'll fix her some ice cream."

THREE

BROOKS BARKER

Brooks Barker, by nature, was not an overly-friendly person, but he was trying his damnedest. As Layla sat at a dining room table in the next room with her headphones on, alternating her attention between the Neapolitan ice cream and her tablet, the two men spoke.

"How'd you end up with a name like Lefty?" asked Brooks. "You left-handed?"

"I'm sure there's a story there, but I don't know it. And no, I'm not left-handed."

"But it's a nickname, right? Not your birth name?"

"No, my real name is Markaveous."

Brooks made a disapproving face. "I'd stick with Lefty." He thought for a minute and then asked, "Spook is gone then?"

"A few years back."

"How'd he go?"

"Cancer. Had it in his lungs. Musta been the smoking."

Brooks nodded. "The man did enjoy his Pall Malls. I'd swear he loved them more than he loved pussy, and that's saying something because Spook Collins lived for pussy."

40

Lefty grinned. "I'd probably be more inclined to appreciate that fact if it hadn't been for the amount of cheating he did on my mom. God only knows how many brothers and sisters I got running around out there that I've never even met."

"Did he go fast?"

"No, he didn't," said Lefty. "He lingered for a couple years. It was bad. Real bad. The man wasted away. He'd always been a big man, but there at the end he weighed less than a hundred pounds. At the end he just stayed there in the hospital. They wouldn't let him go home. He was so doped up he didn't know if he was coming or going, but you know what? The pain was so strong, so intense, even with all those meds, he would scream out in pain. He kept trying to pull out his catheter and his IV. The pain was making him crazy and he would try to fight the nurses. It was a terrible thing to watch him reduced to that. But I sat there with him, day in and day out, as much as I possibly could. I watched him die just a little bit at a time. It was rough. It was really hard on him."

"And your mother?" asked Brooks.

"She bailed a few years before that. I guess she'd had enough of his shit. My pops wasn't always the easiest man to be around. He was mean when he was in the best of moods, and the best of moods didn't occur often. And he drank way too much."

"Rum and Coke?" asked Brooks.

"To the very end. I'm surprised they weren't pumping that shit through his IV."

Brooks chuckled. "Your old man was a pain in the ass. That's what he was. I'd like to say otherwise, but I can't."

"You guys didn't talk for a lot of years. Can I ask what happened? He never would say. Was it a woman?"

Brooks looked at him. "I guess you could say this was about a woman, but not the way you think. It was Dixie, my ex-wife. Her and Spook, they were like oil and water, only in their case the oil was on fire. You ever see that shit, where there's oil in the water and they light it on fire? Well, that's how it was with those two. They couldn't see eye to eye on anything. And that wasn't all Spook's fault. That woman was as tough as they come. I mean, she was really tough. Sometimes she would get mad at me and I wouldn't even know she was mad until she hit me in the head with a pot or a pan—whatever she could get ahold of."

Lefty chuckled. "She might have been tough, but my dad had a problem with women in general. He didn't think much of them, and he didn't like them telling him what to do."

"Yeah, that was him alright."

"But you know, he thought the world of you."

Brooks was visibly surprised. "He said that?"

"He used to tell me all the time that if I ever needed a hitter to go out on a job with me, I should go to Tulsa and find Brooks Barker," said Lefty. "He said you were the best hitter he ever saw. He said he was good, better than good even, but he said you were the best. When he spoke of you, he always spoke with reverence, like he was talking about Jesus himself."

"The part about him telling you to come to Tulsa to find me," said Brooks. "Is that why you're here now?"

"It is," said Lefty. "But this isn't just any job. This is the mother of all jobs. In fact, this is mother of the mother of the mother of all jobs. The job to end all jobs. It's the opportunity of a lifetime, the kind of job you either take or you spend the rest of your life regretting not taking."

Brooks raised his mug, taking a sip of his whiskey-infused coffee. "I don't do that stuff anymore. I'm not a hitter anymore. I'm retired from all that."

"I knew you were gonna say that."

"That's how it is," said Brooks. "Killing's a young man's game."

"It doesn't have to be," said Lefty. "What if you could make one last score? Enough to get straight for the rest of your life?"

"There's a cliché. 'One last score.' You know how many movies there are about criminals trying to make one last score? There's more movies like that than there are grains of sand in the Sahara. And you know what? That one last score stuff is silly. It's a pipe dream that never works out for anybody. There's only two ways a man ever makes one last score—he either dies or he gets locked up. That's it. There ain't no happy endings in this life, kid."

"This job's different. This is the big one."

"How much are we talkin' about?"

"Two million."

Brooks stared at him in disbelief. "Two million dollars? For one fucking guy?"

"For one fucking guy."

"Why's it so damned high? This guy musta really done something to piss off someone important."

"It appears so," said Lefty. "This is why you never piss off rich people."

"Words to live by," said Brooks. "So you're in the life now? Like your old man?"

"I guess you could say I went into the family business."

"Why would you do that? I can see you're a bright kid, had other options. Why would you wanna pick up a gun and do all this?"

"The work just appealed to me," said Lefty. "My father

43

would tell me these stories about hits you guys used to do, different jobs he'd pulled, marks he'd killed. It just appealed to me. The money is good. I don't have a college degree. I tried, but I never could get past college algebra. I took that motherfucker three times, and it got the best of me every time. Without a degree, there isn't much I'm qualified to do, and certainly nothing that pays what a hitter makes. And I don't wanna settle for some rinky-dink no-pay job. I'm not flipping burgers for a living."

"So you actually like this line of work?"

"The answer should be no," said Lefty. "I'm fully aware of that. But having said that, I don't mind it. In fact, I actually kinda like it. It's perverse, I guess, but it gives me a rush, killing someone. And there aren't a lot of other jobs like that. Here you can kill somebody and not feel like you're doing something immoral."

"You don't think it's immoral, killing someone?"

"Of course it's immoral," said Lefty. "But not in the way it is for someone like Jeffrey Dahmer or John Wayne Gacy. They're just out hacking up people like firewood, and maybe eatin' 'em with A-1 sauce or whatever. But not us. Not a hitter. That's not what we do. We're like the soldier in the Marines who goes off to Vietnam and kills gooks in the war. He's just doing his job. He's got nothing against those people. It's just business. It's what he does, so he does it. And at the end of each day, he gets to go home and look at himself in the mirror and not hate what he sees there."

"Do you like what you see when you look in the mirror?" asked Brooks.

"Nobody's perfect. Maybe Jesus if you believe in that kind of thing, which I don't. But I'm not perfect. Not me, not you. I do my best. I take care of that little girl in there, and I put my best foot forward and try to be the best person I can be."

Brooks grinned. "A good person who just happens to murder people."

"You asked me why I liked the job? The hours are good and the pay is great. I barely work at all, and I got a nice house and a brand new Cadillac. Me and the little one always got food on our table and I can afford to pay the spic kid who lives next door to come over and mow the yard every week. I'm living the goddamn American dream. I had to kill a few people to get there, but that's the price of admission."

"I killed my fair share, I guess."

Lefty laughed. "You killed more than that. You put a whole bunch of people in the ground. You probably coulda filled an entire cemetery. You're a goddamn legend, Brooks."

"I suppose so," said Brooks. "But all that's over now."

"But you miss it. I can hear it in your voice."

"So where is this job, anyway?"

"It's in Detroit."

"Detroit?" asked Brooks, the disdain clear in his voice. "Goddamn place is like Beirut, only not as nice. It's a fucking eyesore. It wasn't really all that great to start with, before the GM plant shut down. But now, after that, it's one big crack-infested shithole. Hiroshima, the day after they dropped the bomb, looked better than fucking Detroit."

"Maybe," said Lefty. "But I think I can stand it for a day or so if I'm getting a million dollars to be there."

Brooks nodded. "Yeah, that's an awful lot of money."

"So you'll do it?"

"I'm considering it. And you know, I haven't killed anybody in a long time. It wouldn't hurt me to get another notch or two on my belt."

45

"When was the last time you killed somebody?"

Brooks looked off into space for a moment, trying to remember. "I suppose it was eight or nine years ago. Some peckerhead cut me off in traffic and flipped me the bird. It takes a lot to piss me off, but that sonofabitch did it. I'm not a bad guy, but there's no call for that. Lots of people piss me off, from the kid that throws my newspaper in the bushes to the dickhead that doesn't use his turn signal. But I don't shoot 'em. You can't just go around shootin' folks willy-nilly. It takes a certain kind of asshole for me to shoot 'em."

"And he was the kind," said Lefty.

Brooks nodded. "When I chased him down and stopped him, he probably could have apologized and talked his way out of it. Like I said, I'm not a bad guy. But no, he didn't do that. He said things about my mother. He called her a whore, said something about dicks in her ass. My mother's been in her grave for a long, long time, so I didn't like that. If Spook ever told you anything about me, I'm sure he told you that I don't fuck around like that."

"So you shot the guy?"

"In the face. Then I tossed him into the dumpster behind Blockbuster."

"Then what?"

"Then I went home," said Brooks.

"Did you lose any sleep?"

"Not one goddamn wink. You know why? Some motherfuckers got it coming. That's just the way it is, kid. He just pushed my buttons on the wrong day at the wrong time. I think about it now, it could have gone different on a different day. Who can say? But I did it. I shot the guy, and I don't feel one way or another about it."

"You ever think about the mark's family when you do a

job?" asked Lefty. "You know, the guy's wife and kids, that kind of stuff?"

"When you're doing what we do, you can't allow yourself to think like that. When you start to see the mark as a human being, it becomes harder to do your job. What about you? Do you think about those things?"

"Sometimes. I try not to, but the thoughts do pop into my head."

"You gotta avoid that. It's not healthy."

"Thing is, one time I shot a guy and his wife. I don't know who the guy was, what he'd done. You know, it's not our job to know those things. We just pull the trigger. But the man and wife, they were taking a shower. I didn't even know she was in there until the moment of truth."

"So you shot her?"

"I had no choice," said Lefty. "But then, when I was leaving, I heard a little girl crying in the next room."

"A little girl?"

"She was only about two. And thanks to me, she didn't have any parents. Her mommy and daddy had gone on to receive their great reward. So there was just her, alone in the world."

Brooks thought about it. Then he looked at Layla. Then he looked back at Lefty.

Lefty nodded. "Wasn't nothing else I could do. I wasn't gonna leave her there."

"So you took her home and raised her as your own."

"I did."

"Damn, kid. You're really something."

"That good or bad?" asked Lefty.

"I'm not sure yet." Brooks sat there quietly for a moment before saying, "Sell me on this job. I mean, I know you want the money, but why? What are you gonna do with your share?"

Lefty thought it over. "Everyone always talks that talk about doing one last score. Most times it never works out or they blow all the money and have to come back and work again. They do like all the rockstars do and get rich and just piss it all away. Or maybe it's just in their blood and they can't walk away. But not me. I'm ready to quit. I wanna make this one last score, for Layla. I want to be able to walk away so I can take care of her, both in terms of parental commitment but also financially. This one is Layla's score."

"You're a good man, Lefty. You're like a priest, only without the kiddie diddling. You're too good for this life."

"That's why I want out. Will you come with me?"

Brooks sighed. "Let me think about it for a bit. For the time being, why don't we talk about something else."

"What do you wanna talk about?"

"Hell if I know, kid."

"What do you do these days, Brooks? How do you fill your days?"

"I listen to music sometimes."

"What kind of music do you like?"

"Lots of stuff," said Brooks. "I listen to a lot of Joe Cocker."

"Okay," said Lefty. "You wanna hear my thoughts on Joe Cocker?"

Brooks grinned. "You've got thoughts on Joe Cocker?"

"What? You think because I'm black I won't have thoughts about the man?"

"Could be. I honestly didn't think colored people listened to Joe Cocker. I haven't spent much time with many colored people other than Spook. I got nothing against them, but that's just the way it's worked out. But you've got thoughts about Joe Cocker?"

"I believe, with every fiber of my being, that both 'Feeling Alright' and 'You Can Leave Your Hat On' need to be put on moratorium immediately. I think this should be done for the good of all mankind."

Brooks laughed. "Why is that?"

"'Feeling Alright' has been overused to the point of ridiculousness. Really, it's way beyond overkill at this point. Anytime they make a movie or a commercial that's geared towards Baby Boomers, they play that goddamn song. I haven't seen this, so I don't know this to be a one-hundred percent bonafide fact, but I would be willing to bet you that Cadillac I got sitting out front that there's a commercial somewhere for adult diapers that uses 'Feeling Alright.' I'm certain that exists."

"That's not a thing," said Brooks.

"It's completely a thing. And not only is it annoying to see and hear, but it's also degrading to both Cocker and the goddamn song. Imagine him sitting there in the studio, pouring his heart out into this thing, this work of art, just to have it put in a commercial for some dumb thing like Chevy trucks or Burger King."

"Okay," said Brooks. "And the other one?"

"'You Can Leave Your Hat On,' along with Marvin Gaye's 'Let's Get It On,' are the most overused 'sexy' songs on the planet. I mean, maybe not the planet. I don't know. Maybe just here. There are lots of Asians and Hindus or whatever. Maybe they got some so-called sexy songs that are used more, but we don't hear about them here. What we hear is 'You Can Leave Your Hat On.' And the point remains, those songs are completely overused and have, in the process, been artistically neutered."

"Their balls have been cut off?"

Lefty nodded. "Their balls have been completely removed. Any bite these songs ever had is now a distant memory thanks to this wrongheaded misuse. That's why I believe those songs should be put out of their misery. It doesn't have to be forever, but we should definitely give them a break. I think they've earned it."

"Interesting," said Brooks, nodding. "And you said you don't believe in Jesus?"

"He needs a moratorium placed on him, too. If he existed, and that's a big if, mind you, historians didn't think enough of him to even record a single word about him. And I don't mean the Bible, but actual records from the time. And this was a man who was executed as an enemy of the state and supposedly rose from the dead. Somehow no one found those events significant enough to record. I find that more than a little bit suspicious, but the reason I bring it up is because we've now done a complete 360 and he's mentioned *everywhere*. You can't go into a gas station without seeing tracts. You can't go into a public bathroom and take a shit without seeing Bible verses scrawled on the stall. I don't know about you, but I don't wanna think about Jesus while I'm taking a shit."

Brooks laughed. "I don't wanna think about anyone while I'm taking a shit."

"Precisely my point. It's not that I got anything against Jesus, per se. I'm sure if he existed he was a cool guy, had his good qualities or whatever, but come on, man, I'm trying to take a shit here. I don't need to know that Kilroy was there or that I can call Linda for a good time. And most of all I don't need to read about the divinity of Jesus. Not then, not there. I just wanna take my shit in peace."

"You're a funny kid," said Brooks. "You remind me of

your old man. He was a hoot. He was angry and cranky most of the time, but then he would say something that would catch me offguard; something funny that would have me in stitches, cracking up. He was one of a kind. I've never met another man like him."

"Would you want to?"

"Not really," said Brooks. He changed the subject. "Let's talk about this contract in Detroit."

"You're interested?"

"Maybe," said Brooks. "But I wanna know who the mark is."

"The mark's name is Bruno De Lorenzo."

"De Lorenzo? Like the crime boss?"

"Antonio De Lorenzo is his daddy."

"That changes things," said Brooks. "I don't have a long time left to live on this planet, but I don't wanna spend my final years watching over my shoulder, waiting for some gunman who's half my age to pop out and whack me."

"Bruno De Lorenzo's supposed to be a real piece of shit," said Lefty.

"Most of these guys are. What makes this one so special that he's worth two million dollars?"

"He's evil. He's done some objectively bad stuff. You haven't heard about any of that?"

"No," said Brooks. "I've been out of the game for a long time. I left, and I didn't look back. I got no ties whatsoever. What kind of stuff did Bruno De Lorenzo do?"

"Bad stuff," said Lefty. "I mean, really awful shit."

"Like what? Give me an example."

"Alright," said Lefty. "I'll tell you a story I heard..."

FOUR

THE STORY LEFTY HEARD

Bruno De Lorenzo was the talk of the Detroit crime world. He'd had a well-known reputation of being crazy since he was a teenager. Way back then, before he was even old enough to be a gangster, he was already doing gangster shit. During a dispute between the De Lorenzo family and a rival drug kingpin, a then sixteen-year-old Bruno took it upon himself to whack out said kingpin, leaving a messy bloodbath in his wake. He'd lied at the door, somehow managing to gain entrance into the man's lair, and then went inside and murdered six people, including the boss, leaving their brains spattered on the walls like some kind of grotesque Jackson Pollock art display. As he grew older, Bruno's thirst for blood became more and more insatiable.

At the age of twenty-two he'd shoved a beloved Mafioso captain from a balcony in a dispute over a questionable call during a World Series game the two were watching together. Most of the De Lorenzo crime family had been outraged over the incident, but Don Antonio had stepped in, defending his crazy offspring. In the years to come, Bruno became the *enfant terrible* of the crime world.

Stories of Bruno raping women and torturing enemy mobsters were a dime a dozen, many of them completely embellished or exaggerated at the least. But a great many of the stories were true. Bruno De Lorenzo had become the boogeyman, a mythologized figure whose powers for evil were discussed and analyzed, making him a crime world legend for all the wrong reasons. He became fodder for jokes, but no one ever dared speak them in his presence, for if they did, everyone was fully aware of what the outcome would be.

Bruno was given free reign to do as he pleased in the Detroit crime world, and he made the most of it, controlling a stable of prostitutes, overseeing collections for his father's business, and operating as an extremely-successful loan shark. In this last endeavor he'd become known as a man you didn't want to miss a payment to. If you did, the results were generally unfavorable to say the least.

Joe Abelli, a longtime associate of Don Antonio's, had pushed his luck to the max, missing not one but two payments to Bruno. It was a modern day miracle Abelli had survived the first non-payment with his limbs and digits intact, but his missing a second payment all but ensured a reprisal.

"You got big balls, Joe," Bruno said, standing over him, wielding a Roberto Clemente-signature ball bat. They were in Bruno's swanky 22nd floor penthouse, where Abelli was sitting on a plush leather ottoman, fearing for his life. By this point Bruno's goons, Pino and Dom, had already beaten the living hell out of the fifty-two-year-old Abelli, cracking and possibly breaking several of his ribs.

But Bruno hadn't killed him. Not yet, and it seriously looked as though Abelli might live to see another cannoli. But he wasn't out of the woods yet, not by a long shot.

Should he survive the day, there would be a time for rejoicing later, but this wasn't it.

"You needed a loan," said Bruno. "You pissed away all your money betting on the ponies down at Hazel Park. But you didn't go to the bank to get that loan, did you?"

Abelli shook his head. "No, I didn't."

"Why didn't you go to the bank, Joe?"

"Because they wouldn't give me the money."

"Right," said Bruno. "They wouldn't give your sorry ass the money. But wasn't it also because you didn't want your wife to know how much you lost? Let's call a nigger a nigger here. Call it what it is. That was the real reason, wasn't it, Joe? If you got a legitimate, above-board loan from a reputable financial institution, she'd find out what a miserable no-good piece of shit you are. I mean, why else would anyone risk borrowing money from a crazy fuck like me?"

Bruno laughed at his joke while Abelli nodded in agreement.

But Bruno wasn't satisfied. "Say it. Say the fuckin' words, Joe."

"You're right," said Abelli. "I didn't want her to know."

"So you came to me."

"I came to you."

Bruno grinned. "How you feeling about that decision now, Joe? You still feel like that was a good idea? That workin' out good for you?" Bruno pointed the barrel of the bat at him. "But back to the point at hand... I graciously...out of the goodness of my own heart...loaned you the money you needed, did I not?"

"You did."

"You're right, I did," agreed Bruno. "$20,000 cash. But now, when it comes time for you to pay the vig, you got nothin' for me. That's kinda fucked up, Joe. This feels like a one-sided friendship. Here I am, taking you out to the movies and dinner, giving you roses and chocolates, but you ain't got no pussy for me. That's real fucked up, Joe." Bruno looked over at his goons. "Isn't that fucked up, guys?"

Pino and Dom both grinned. Abelli stared up at Bruno, blinking, but not pushing his luck so far as to speak.

"This is the second time you haven't had my money," said Bruno. He looked over at Pino and Dom again, putting on a show for them. "After I gave you the money, you got nothin' for me. I find that offensive, Joe. I find that down-right unfortunate. I mean, who does that, Joe? Who the fuck does that?"

Abelli said nothing.

"I'll bet you had the money, too, didn't you, Joe? I'll bet you had the money set aside to pay me, and then... What did you do, Joe? You went back to the track, didn't you? You went back down there and lost all your money again, didn't you?"

Abelli started to cry. He didn't want to cry, but that didn't stop the tears from flowing. "I didn't go to the track."

Bruno was startled by Abelli's audacity. He leaned forward. *"What did you say?"*

"I didn't take the money to the track."

"But you had it, right?" said Bruno. "At some point you had the money set aside to pay me, didn't you?"

Abelli nodded.

"What did you do with it, Joe?"

Abelli looked up. "Lottery tickets."

Bruno looked at him, not believing what he was hearing. "You bought lottery tickets with the money?"

"I did."

"That's a lot of goddamn lottery tickets," said Bruno.

"And you still didn't win anything? That's some real piss-poor luck you got, Joe."

Abelli said, "I won some free tickets."

Bruno looked at him as though he was the dumbest piece of shit on the planet. "What do you think I should do here? If you were me, what would you do in my situation? How would you handle this little bit of fuckery you've presented me with?"

Abelli considered it. "I'd give me another chance."

Bruno chuckled, looking up at the goons, encouraging them to laugh, as well. They did. "Somehow I knew you'd say that, Joe. Somehow I knew that shit. I must be psychic or somethin'." He paused for a moment, starting to pace, thumping the barrel of the bat against his open palm. "You don't think I should break all your bones?" He stared at Abelli, expecting an answer. "Should I crush in your skull?"

"No, I don't think so."

Bruno looked at him with a tired expression on his face. "Why is that, Joe? Tell me why I shouldn't bash your head in. I'm all ears."

Abelli struggled to find an answer, eventually landing on, "If you kill me, you won't get your money."

Bruno nodded. "Good a reason as any, I guess. Not entirely accurate, but we'll go with that. I'll tell you what, Joe. I'm feeling magnanimous today. I'm gonna let you slide this time, with no broken bones. With your life intact. What do you say about that?"

Abelli started to cry harder. "Thank you, Bruno. Thank you."

"But I'm gonna need you to do something for me."

"Anything," said Abelli. "Just name it."

"You got a daughter, correct?"

Abelli was instantly stricken with fear. "I got two daughters."

"The little one," said Bruno. "How old is the youngest one?"

"That's Jess. She just turned eleven."

"I want you to bring her up here to see me. I wanna have a talk with her."

Abelli bit his lip, worried. "Why?"

"I wanna tell her some things about her degenerate fucking gambler father. That okay with you?"

"You promise you won't hurt her?"

Bruno looked over at Pino and Dom. "What? You think I'm in the business of hurtin' kids, Joe? What kind of guy do you think I am? Do I strike you as the kind of guy who goes around hurtin' kids? If I crossed my heart and hoped to die, would that ease your mind?"

Abelli said nothing, afraid of saying the wrong thing.

"I'm guessing you've heard some stuff about me. Tell me, Joe, what have you heard? What's the word on the street about Bruno De Lorenzo?"

Abelli struggled. "I just heard you can be..."

"*Cruel?*" Bruno asked, a twisted smile on his face.

Abelli nodded.

"Tell you what, Joe. If you don't bring your daughter Jess to come and see me, you're gonna find out what cruelty really means. Your whole family will. I'll bring such great pain and suffering down on your house that you'll think Job had it good. You remember Job, from the Bible?"

"Yeah."

"God did all kinds of fucked up shit to that man. Gave him worms, killed his kids, killed his livestock, destroyed his crops... And you know what? That's not even close to what I'll do to your ass—to the collective asses of every single

57

person you love—if you don't do what I ask and bring that little girl to come and see me. *Capeesh?*"

Abelli nodded. "I got it."

Bruno looked at him. "Do you?"

"I'll bring her to you."

ABELLI SPENT the next day seriously contemplating suicide. He had dug himself into a hole he now feared he would not be able to climb out of. The determining factor of his deciding not to take his own life was the realization that such an act would not stop Bruno's wrath against his family, and would probably even motivate him to inflict more damage. So, against his better judgment, Abelli decided to just get it over with and bring Jess to see the man.

As they rode on the elevator, some crap music playing in there, Abelli prepared the little girl. "We are going to meet a man today," he said. "He's going to talk to you. But... I should tell you he's going to say some bad things about your father. That's just the way it is, there's nothing we can do about it. So you just do me a favor and don't say anything back to him unless he asks you a question. Try not to get upset by what he says, and when we're finished, I'll take you to that ice cream parlor you like..."

She perked up at this. Now he was speaking her language. She looked at him, her eyes big. "We'll go to Ice Cream Dream?"

Abelli nodded. "Just me and you, kid. I'll let you get whatever you want."

"I want pineapple ice cream."

"Pineapple ice cream then."

"With gummy bears on top."

"Sure," Abelli said. "Lots of gummy bears."

"And Fruity Pebbles."

"Right," he said, nodding again. "Sounds good."

"Yum," she said, smiling.

"But let's talk about this man for a moment. He's not a very nice man."

"Then why are we talking to him?"

"That's a good question," said Abelli. "But Daddy works with him. He's like a boss, and sometimes bosses aren't very nice people. Sometimes they're dicks."

She looked at him solemnly. "Is that a bad word?"

"Yes, it is. It's a grown-up word. Only grown-ups can say that one."

"Okay," she said, considering it. "Can I say it when I'm a grown-up?"

"Sure. You can say anything you want when you're a grown-up. So what are you gonna do if this man says mean things?"

"Try not to get upset and don't talk unless he asks me a question."

"Good girl," said Abelli. "You do that and we'll get out of there a whole lot faster. It'll all be finished in no time. Then—"

"*Ice Cream Dream!*" she interjected.

"Pineapple ice cream with gummy bears and Fruity Pebbles." The elevator door opened on the 22nd floor. Abelli braced himself for the impending interaction. Perhaps Bruno would take it easy on him since there was a child present. Maybe it would all be fine.

"Come on," Abelli said, leading Jess to Bruno's door. He knocked. He could hear no movement inside and was momentarily excited by the prospect of no one being home. But Pino answered the door, waving them inside.

Bruno was walking around in silk boxer shorts, wearing

a silky purple robe that was open in front. "Come on in," he welcomed. "I see you brought your daughter. Lovely child. What's her name again?"

"My name is Jess," said the girl happily.

Bruno grinned. "Nice to meet you, Jess."

"Likewise," she said.

"How's school going?" asked Bruno.

Jess looked at her father, and then back at Bruno. "School is good."

"You like school?"

"I love school."

"Not me," said Bruno. "I hated school when I was a kid. But good for you, Jess." He turned and looked at Dom. "Bring me one of the stools from the bar." Dom nodded and went to fetch the stool, bringing it to Bruno.

Bruno took the stool in one hand and placed it in the center of the room. He looked at Jess. "Come here," he said. "I'd like you to sit here."

Jess looked at her father, who was visibly terrified. The smile still on her face, Jess moved slowly towards the stool. She sat down, facing her father. Bruno motioned towards the ottoman. "Have a seat, Joe." Abelli did this reluctantly. Bruno looked at Dom and nodded. Dom disappeared for a moment, reemerging with a pump shotgun. He walked around in front of Abelli, standing over him. He racked the thing, letting Abelli know he meant business. Abelli squirmed uneasily but said nothing.

Bruno stroked Jess' long black hair, looking up at Joe as he did this. "You're a real pretty girl, Jess," he said, sounding every bit as creepy as he'd intended. Bruno leaned in towards the girl and kissed her ear. "You remind me of a girlfriend I had when I was a kid," Bruno said. Abelli didn't like this one bit. "Her name was Lisa," Bruno continued. "I lost my virginity when I was twelve. My father took me to a whore house on my birthday. But it was different for Lisa. She hadn't lost her virginity yet." Bruno looked at Joe, trying to tempt him to attack. "She didn't lose her virginity until she met me."

Bruno, behind Jess, moved her hair aside, kissing her neck. Jess was terribly uncomfortable. She looked at her father, but he couldn't help her. Both of them squirmed.

"You doing alright over there, Joe?" asked Bruno. "You look uncomfortable. If I didn't know any better, I'd think you were afraid I was going to rape your little girl." He and Joe looked at one another, the expression on Joe's face conveying both terror and a pleading with Bruno not to hurt her.

"Do you honestly think I would hurt your little girl, Joe?" asked Bruno. "Is that what you think?"

Abelli said nothing.

"Let me set your mind at ease, Joe. I'm not gonna rape your daughter. I'm not that kind of man. I don't do that kind of shit." He looked at Pino. "But Pino here is that kind of man. Isn't that right, Pino?" Pino said nothing. "Pino, I'd like you to rape Joe's daughter. Could you do that for me?"

Abelli tried to climb to his feet, but Dom struck him down with the butt of the shotgun, splitting his forehead and knocking him back onto to the ottoman.

Pino came forward, not wanting to rape the girl, but prepared to do as his boss had instructed. "Kiss the girl, Pino." Pino shrugged and kissed her, starting with her forehead. Abelli wept, unable to move without being struck. Bruno stared mostly at Abelli, but occasionally looked over to see the depravity taking place only a few feet away from him. Abelli tried to shield his eyes, but Bruno instructed

Dom to strike him with the shotgun anytime he looked away.

"You're not getting off that easy, Joe," said Bruno. "You're gonna watch that shit. Every bit of it." Bruno was smiling a sick, twisted smile, obviously getting great pleasure from this. "You see that, Joe? What do you think of that? Daddy's little girl is gonna become a woman today. Daddy's girl could be Pino's slut. One man's treasure is another man's trash." Bruno laughed a grating, sadistic laugh.

Abelli glared at him through his tears. *"I'll make you pay for this, Bruno. If it's the last thing I ever do, you'll pay, you sonofabitch!"*

Bruno chuckled. "You think that's how it works, Joe? Life doesn't work like that. Life never works like that. That will never happen. I'm in control here, not you, and certainly not God. Bad things happen to good people, Joe. You remember that? There was a book called *Why Bad Things Happen to Good People*. You know why that is, Joe? You know why those things happen? It's because good people are also weak people who get what they've got coming to them. That's how life works. But bad people? They never really pay. They just don't. Your girl Jess here, she did nothing to deserve any of this. You did this, Joe. Make no mistake, she's going to pay for your sins." Bruno looked over at Jess, whose ear was being kissed by Pino. "You hear that, Jess? This is happening because of your no good piece of shit father. He's the one that did all of this. Please remember, he brought you here."

Abelli wailed.

Pino didn't get beyond kissing the girl's neck before Bruno thankfully put an end to it. "Go ahead and stop, Pino," he said. "I don't want you to rape her." Bruno walked out of the room. Abelli wondered what was happening. Pino was still standing over the weeping girl, attempting to console her, despite having just kissed her. He had his arms wrapped around her, and she was sobbing hard, her head against his shoulder. A moment later Bruno reemerged, carrying a hunting bow and some arrows. Abelli was unsure what was happening, but he knew it wasn't good.

"I've taken up archery," said Bruno. "It's my new hobby. I hadn't really had any hobbies since I was a kid, other than chasing skirt and lifting weights. Jerking off, maybe. Is that considered a hobby?" Bruno chuckled. "But this, archery, gives me perspective. I really enjoy it. How about you? You like archery, Joe? You ever shoot a bow before?"

Exhausted, Abelli said nothing. He wiped away his tears, sitting there in silence.

Bruno stood beside him. "Get back, Pino. Leave Jess alone." Pino looked at his boss and moved away from Jess, leaving her sitting on the bar stool, sobbing.

"I'm not very good at this archery thing yet," said Bruno. "I went to the range, but I couldn't shoot shit. It looks so easy, but man, it's pretty fucking hard. Did you know that, Joe? Were you aware that archery was actually pretty difficult?"

Abelli said nothing.

"I would pull back the bowstring and aim at that target ever so carefully," said Bruno. "But then I'd release the thing and that arrow would fly off somewhere, nowhere close to the intended target. I'm good at lots of things. I always have been. I got natural talents, but I don't think archery is gonna be one of them. But maybe one day. And you know, practice makes perfect." Bruno looked at Joe. "You wanna watch me practice, Joe?"

"Please don't hurt her," Abelli said. "I'll give you anything you want."

This touched a nerve. "Will you now?!" Bruno stared at him. "Like the money you owe me? *Like the money you fucking owe me?* I'm not a bad man, Joe. I mean, well, I guess I am a bad man, but I'm not asking for anything out of line here. You owe me. That's a thing, that's the way it is. Objectively speaking, you owe me money. That's all I want —what I'm owed."

Bruno raised the bow, an arrow carefully placed against it. "This bow has a draw weight of fifty pounds," he said. "Do you know what that means, Joe? That means it's strong enough to take down an elk or a moose. But there ain't no elk or moose around here, Joe. None that I've seen anyway. I've seen a few niggers and some homeless people, but that's about it." He paused, adding, "How much damage do you think this son of a bitch would do to a human being? What do you think it would do to an eleven-year-old girl's face?" Bruno drew back on the bowstring, carefully aiming the arrow at Jess, who was sitting there teary-eyed and motion-less. "They say the key is being steady and careful," said Bruno. "And you gotta breathe real slow." He released the bowstring, and the arrow zipped past Jess' head, breaking a window in the dining room.

"Dammit," Bruno said, chuckling. He looked at the crying girl, squirming uncomfortably, and then at her father. "Looks like a win for you, little girl," he said. "Jess one, Bruno zero. But that can change at any minute."

"Please, Bruno," Abelli begged. "Please don't hurt her."

Bruno was busy replacing the arrow with a second. "Don't be such a crybaby, Joe. It's unbecoming. It makes you look weak. You are weak, but try not to look it so much. It's really embarrassing." He looked at Jess, sitting there crying.

"Do you think it's embarrassing, Jess? Are you embarrassed by how weak a man your father is? I would be if I was you. I really would. He's fuckin' pathetic. How could a man like that ever protect you?"

Bruno raised the bow again, steadying the arrow. "He can't protect you. He's a shitty father, Jess. He's as bad a father as he is a gambler." Bruno stopped to look over at Abelli. "You really are worthless, Joe. You know that, right? There is absolutely no reason for you to exist." When Abelli said nothing, Bruno pushed. "Go ahead and say it, Joe. Tell your little girl what a worthless fuck you are."

Abelli was shaking. He looked at Jess, who was staring at him in search of the savior he could never be. "It's true, Jess. I'm worthless."

"You're a worthless fuck," said Bruno.

"Yeah," said Abelli. "I'm worthless and...I'm...a fuck."

Bruno grinned. "At least he's honest about it, Jess. That's half the battle right there. It's always good when a person can acknowledge his faults, and for him, being a fuck is certainly one of them." Bruno pulled back the bowstring. He released it, and the second arrow zipped through the room, grazing the side of Jess' face. She cried out, startled as much as anything, but she was alright save for an ever-reddening slice across her cheek.

"Would you look at that?" asked Bruno, becoming more animated now. "That was pretty damned amazing. Maybe there is a God, Joe." He looked up at the ceiling. "You think there's a God?"

"Yes," said Abelli. "I believe in God."

"Great," said Bruno. "I want you to do something for me. I want you to pray, right here and now, in front of me. Pray out loud. Ask God to come down and save your little girl, Joe. Would you do that for me?"

Abelli was shaking badly. He pressed his hands together and closed his eyes. His voice trembled. "Dear God in heaven, please, I ask you, please help my Jess. Please. If you do this one thing for me, I'll do anything. I'll stop gambling. I'll go to church. I'll do anything."

Bruno was staring at him, a big sick smile on his face. "Tell him 'please,' Joe."

"Please," said Abelli. "Please save my Jess."

"Now say amen."

"Amen."

"Maybe this was all just part of God's divine plan," said Bruno. "I'll tell you what. I'll shoot one more arrow. Just one. And if it misses her again, the game is over, you two go home and we never talk about any of this again. How does that sound? You'll still owe me the money, but you'll pay it from now on. How does that sound, Joe?"

Abelli managed, "Please...Bruno..."

Bruno looked at Jess, crying hard now. "We're almost done here, kiddo. It's okay. God's coming to save you now. He'll be here in a minute. I'm sure he's just stuck in traffic or something."

He raised the bow once more, steadying the arrow. He drew back the bowstring, and let it rip. The arrow zipped across the room, burying itself in the girl's throat. She made a loud gurgling sound and fell to the floor, writhing there.

"*No!*" screamed Abelli. He tried to stand, but Dom knocked him back onto the ottoman.

Bruno put down the bow, leaning it against the wall, and picked up his glass, nonchalantly taking a drink. He walked towards the dying girl. He stood over her. "It looks like you crapped out. Sorry, kid, I guess God was busy today. I don't think he's coming. But hey, Jess, I need you to remember one thing, just one little thing. Your father did this to you. He's the reason you're dying now. So if you see St. Peter up there, which I very much doubt is gonna happen—probably you'll just be gone—I want you to tell him what a piece of garbage Joe Abelli was. You tell him that, okay?"

Abelli wailed, whimpered, and sobbed, unable to touch his little girl, alive, for the last time, let alone save her.

Bruno looked at him. "Dom, Pino, I want you to bury Joe here alive. You guys get a casket and put him in there. Not some rinky dink wooden box, but an actual factual casket. Then what I want you to do is put some bottles of water in there for him. Maybe five or six, so he'll stay alive for a while. He'll want to die, but he'll end up drinking that water."

"Please, Bruno," said Abelli.

Bruno ignored his pleas. "Then you take his daughter's body and put it in there on top of him. That way, when he fights death and tries to stay alive, he'll have to eat her flesh. He'll still die, but he'll fight it for as long as he can. And whatever you do, don't let him have anything sharp in there that he can use to try to kill himself. No keys, no nothing. Just water and his dead kid. That's it." He looked at Joe, grinning. "Sorry, buddy, you gotta suffer this one out."

"I'll get you, you son of a bitch!" Joe spat. *"You haven't heard the last of me!"*

Bruno sneered. "Unless someone brings a Ouija board to the party, I'm pretty sure I've heard all I'm gonna hear from you. Take care, Joe. *Bon apetite!*"

FIVE

PARTNERS IN CRIME

Brooks stared at Lefty, hanging on his every word. After Lefty had concluded the story by telling him about Bruno burying Abelli with his eleven-year-old daughter, he asked, "Is that true?"

"As far as I know it is."

"How do you know?"

"I don't really, but there are lots of those stories. Really bad, really dark, sadistic stories about the guy torturing and hurting people with a big fat stupid grin plastered across his mug. Those stories are as common as liars in the White House. I've been hearing them for years, and I don't even fuck around in Detroit. The guy is infamous for that shit. So yeah, I believe it. Can I prove it, or do I know it to one-hundred-percent be a fact? No, but obviously the guy is terrible. He's got a two million dollar contract on his head. You don't get a contract that big unless you've done something to really piss somebody off."

"I'm sure you're right," said Brooks, taking another sip of his coffee. "But it sounds ridiculous. It's one of those stories that's so perfect that it almost has to be made up."

"I don't think it is, though."

"I don't either," said Brooks. "He sounds like a swell guy."

"I'm glad I don't work in Detroit."

Brooks looked at him. "But you wanna start now?"

"I wouldn't mind tangling with him as much when he's staring down the barrel of my Glock," said Lefty. "I think that's the only way you can deal with a snake like that. Anything other than that, you're setting yourself up to be buried in a hole and eating your dead kid."

"Christ," said Brooks. "That story, it's really something."

"It's impressively gruesome."

"A guy like that, he's got it coming. Killing someone like him is just doing the world a service. That's a humanitarian effort, done for the good of the universe."

Lefty nodded. "I think you're right."

"I've decided."

Lefty perked up.

"I'll do it," said Brooks. "I'll do it just for the pleasure of taking out a piece of shit like that." He looked at the younger hitman. "But that doesn't mean I don't want my share of the money, so don't go making plans on what you're gonna do with it."

Lefty grinned. "I figured as much."

"I'll do it," said Brooks, "but only on one condition."

"There's a condition?"

"There's a condition."

"Okay, what is it?"

"I wanna bring someone else in on this."

This caught Lefty offguard. He stiffened. "Who?"

"My old partner. I owe her, and I figure this would repay her. Also, she's the second best hitter I ever worked with. Your old man was the first, but she's a close second."

69

Lefty's eyes narrowed. "Who is this person, Brooks?"

"My ex-wife, Dixie."

"Let me get this straight," said Lefty. "You wanna bring your ex-wife?"

Brooks nodded. "We could use the help."

Lefty mulled it over. "You sure about this?"

"It's the only way I'll do it." Brooks looked at him, his expression a serious one. "I'm sure you can handle it without me, but if you want me on this, she comes with us."

"I wasn't prepared for a third person."

"Well, I wasn't prepared for you to show up on my doorstep asking me to go to Detroit to kill the son of a mob boss, but here you are. Not wanting a thing, or not being prepared for it, that doesn't change it from happening."

"That's how it is?"

Brooks nodded solemnly. "That's how it is."

"And she's good?"

"She's better than good," said Brooks. "Dixie's the best there is now that Spook is gone."

"Is she better than you?"

Brooks grinned. "Let's not get carried away. She's good, but..."

"But not as good as you?"

"I don't brag. I'm a pretty humble guy, but sometimes when you're good at a thing it's okay to acknowledge it. It's not being cocky if it's true."

"And?"

"I'm the best," said Brooks flatly. "I don't know a lot of these new guys, so maybe there's someone who's better now, but I don't know him."

Lefty looked at him and said, "How do you know I'm not the guy?"

"If you really wanna know, it's because of her," said Brooks, pointing at Layla. "She weighs you down. To be really good at this, you can't have emotional baggage. You can't love anyone. It doesn't work like that. Those things are mutually exclusive."

"But what about your ex-wife?" asked Lefty. "You loved her?"

"I'm not sure I did. I respected her, and I liked her a lot, but I don't think I loved her. That's not a knock against her, but by the time we met we'd both killed more people than we'd really ever known in life. We were both cold and removed. Neither one of us was a warm, loving person. Because we were stone cold killers. We didn't get attached. We both knew better. So that little girl in there? I'm glad she's got you to take care of her, and I'm happy for you. But to be really great at this thing, you can't have emotional ties. You can't have anyone in your life that you're not willing to either walk away from or put into the ground without hesitation."

Lefty said, "That's pretty bleak."

"Life is bleak," said Brooks. "But our life—*the crime life* —is even more so. That guy in your story, that Abelli? He deserved what he got in a way."

"How you figure that?"

"Because he had no business being in that line of work with young kids at home. He put them in danger. If I was the boss, I wouldn't even hire guys like that. They're a liability."

Lefty looked him in the eyes. "It sounds like you're judging me."

"I'm sorry it sounds that way," said Brooks. "But I'm not. Not at all. I'm happy for you. I'm sure you're good at what you do. You seem like a bright kid. But I don't think you can

ANDY RAUSCH

ever be the best and truly live up to your full potential with that kid in tow."

"You mentioned people like that being a liability," said Lefty. "Why would you work with me if you felt that way?"

"I get a good vibe from you. I think you're a good guy and I think your heart is in the right place. And I won't be putting myself in a position where I could be damaged by you or your baggage. I watch out for myself. I'll be fine. And I don't think you're gonna try to double-cross me like a lot of guys will, not with your kid being there with us."

Lefty nodded and changed the subject. "Are you prepared to split your share of the money with Dixie?"

"No, I'm not. Do you want me on this job?"

"Absolutely. That's why I'm here in goddamn Tulsa, Oklahoma. Do you think I want to be in fucking Oklahoma? Cause I'll answer that for you real quick—the answer is no, I don't want to be in fucking Oklahoma. There are only two things I give a shit about in Tulsa, and both of those places are apparently gone now. But I came to talk to you, Brooks, so yes, I want you on this job."

"Then Dixie gets a full share."

"She gets a third?" asked Lefty, irritated.

"She gets a full third."

Lefty thought about this. "$666,000 is less than a million dollars."

"Last time I checked, yeah, it is. But it's still a lot of money."

Lefty looked at Layla sitting at the table playing on her tablet. He considered doing the job alone and keeping all the money himself, but he wasn't sure he could do it alone. And there was Layla to consider. She needed him, so he couldn't afford to take unnecessary chances.

Brooks saw him looking at her. "Are you sure you

72

wanna take her? I mean, this man, this Bruno De Lorenzo character, apparently has no problem killing little girls."

Lefty looked at him, serious now. "She stays with me. The thought occurred to me, absolutely, but I'm all she's got. She needs me. And if I'm being completely honest, I need her. I think I've become co-dependent on her. You know how a heroin junkie can't function without that smack in his system? That's how I am with Layla. If I don't have her, I don't know how to function. And if that makes me less at this job like you say it does, then fine. I'm getting out after this job anyway."

"But will she be safe?" asked Brooks.

"I'll do everything I can to make sure she is," said Lefty. "Rest assured I'll take care of that little girl. Anybody tries to hurt her..."

"What?"

"They die, simple as that. And they don't just die, they die really fucking badly. They die the kind of death the bad guy dies at the end of a Bruce Willis action movie. The kind that makes the audience cheer and go nuts. That's how they get it, on some Medieval shit, violent and gruesome. I'll make that shit Bruno did to Abelli look like child's play."

Brooks didn't doubt it. "So Dixie?"

Lefty considered the matter. After a minute or so passed he said, "What the hell? Bring her along."

"She gets a full share?"

Lefty nodded. "Full share."

Brooks put out his hand for Lefty to shake. Lefty smiled. "We're doing this now?"

"This is how it's done."

Lefty shook his hand, thankful Brooks didn't do any of that silly macho white guy stuff where he squeezed his hand as tight as he could to prove how tough he was.

"One thing," said Lefty.

"What's that?"

Lefty put his hand up, making a fist. He extended it towards Brooks, who looked at it as though it were a foreign thing.

"What am I supposed to do here?"

Lefty chuckled. "Make a fist."

Brooks did. Lefty extended his fist toward Brooks. "Bump my fist." Brooks did, not completely sure what was happening.

"This is what they do now?" asked Brooks.

"This is how it's done."

"Is that a colored people thing?"

Lefty grinned. "Old man, this is a new day. That's an everybody thing. Everybody bumps fists. Even crusty old crackers like you."

"Knock off that old man shit, kid," said Brooks. "I'd hate for you to get killed by a crusty old cracker in front of your kid."

And so it began.

LEFTY WAS NOT enthusiastic about the addition of the old man's ex-wife. Brooks informed him that Dixie lived in Oklahoma City. Lefty was thankful that she only lived two hours away from Tulsa, as he wouldn't have wanted to waste extra time driving somewhere far away to get get her.

"You gonna call her?" asked Lefty.

"No," Brooks said, shaking his head. "We don't really do the phone thing."

"Shouldn't she probably know we're coming?"

"If I called her, she wouldn't talk to me."

"You guys don't get along?"

"She's my *ex-wife*, kid. How do you think we get along? That's why she's my ex-wife."

"But you think she'll do it?" asked Lefty.

"I do," said Brooks. "Last I knew she was working this stupid, dead-end job there in Oklahoma City. She'll jump at the chance to make that much money for a couple days' worth of work. Besides, she's like us."

"What do you mean?"

"Being a hitter is in her blood."

"It's not in my blood," said Lefty. "I'm trying to get out."

Brooks grinned at him knowingly. "You say that now... Thing is, you can get out of the life, but that don't mean you can get the life out of you."

It was agreed that they would ride together to meet Dixie in Lefty's Cadillac. Brooks packed his bags fairly quickly. "I've still got one last thing to do," he said.

"What's that?"

"You're gonna have to help me dig."

"Dig?" asked Lefty, not wanting to dig.

"When I quit, I buried my weapons in a box in the backyard. Everything but the .45 I carry for safety. So I need my guns before I can do this thing."

Lefty sighed. "Alright, I'll help you dig. But I'm not doing it all. You're gonna have to do some digging, too."

Brooks smiled. "You're not afraid of wearing out an old man? I mean, if I die out there digging, you're gonna have to go by yourself."

"I'll take my chances. I think your old ass will be just fine."

BROOKS ONLY OWNED ONE SHOVEL, and Lefty carried it. Once they were outside, leaving Layla in the living room

ANDY RAUSCH

watching *Spongebob*, Lefty looked around the sad little yard. It was mostly empty, save for an old rusty frame for a swing set that no longer held any swings. The grass was freshly cut, the sure sign of an old man with too much time on his hands. Lefty thought of his neighbor back in Chicago. The old man got up twice a week and started mowing his yard before the sun even started to rise. Lefty wondered if Brooks did that. Was that a universal old man thing? There was an old dilapidated wooden privacy fence surrounding the yard. The fact that it was even still standing was possible proof that miracles existed.

"Watch out for snakes," said Brooks. "I get a lot of 'em out here."

Lefty hated snakes. "Jesus Christ," he muttered. "What kind of snakes?"

"How the hell do I know? Do I look like a snake expert?"

"Well, what do they look like?"

"They look like snakes," said Brooks. "What the hell do you think they look like? They're slimy-looking little bastards. My favorite thing in the world is to run over them on my riding mower and chop them to pieces. Then they go flying out the side of the mower with the cut grass. That kind of amuses me."

"I thought you didn't kill anymore."

"I make exceptions for snakes," said Brooks.

"But you don't know what kind they are?"

Brooks looked at him, an irritated look on his face. "They're the kind that slither around and scare the shit out of me. Someone told me they were garden snakes, but I don't know if that's their proper name."

"I didn't think you were scared of anything."

"You got a lot to learn, kid," said Brooks. "I'm scared of lots of things."

"Like what? What scares Brooks Barker?"

Brooks thought about it for a second. "Women. They're scary. You know what's even scarier? Living with them. That's scary shit for sure."

Lefty nodded. "That's the truth."

"I'm afraid of dying... Don't get me wrong, I do what I have to do when I'm out there doing a job. It's not so much the act of dying that scares me as the actual being dead part. I'm not a big fan of that, the being gone."

"Do you believe in heaven?" asked Lefty.

"You ask a lot of questions, kid."

"I guess it's my nature."

"You're a pain in the ass, just like your old man. You know, I'd like to believe in heaven, but I don't know. My first wife, Bernice, died when we she was twenty-three. I like to think maybe she's up in heaven, waiting for me, but I don't really know what I believe anymore. I think that's okay, though. Because whether or not heaven does or does not exist is not gonna change because of what you or I believe. How about you? Do you believe in heaven?"

"No," said Lefty. "But I want to."

"I guess you gotta fake it till you make it."

Brooks led Lefty to the skeletal remains of the swing set. "I buried the guns under there."

"Why do you have a swing set?"

"When I get bored I go out and swing," said Brooks dryly.

"You wouldn't get too far without swings."

Brooks just looked at him.

"So where did you get the idea to bury the guns?" asked Lefty.

"I saw it in a movie, I think."

"You always do what you see in movies?" asked Lefty. "Do me a favor, Brooks. Don't watch *Silence of the Lambs*. I don't want you to start eating people."

"I mostly only watch westerns," said Brooks. "John Wayne, Randolph Scott."

"John Wayne has a movie where he buries guns?"

"I don't know," said Brooks. "He might though."

"We've only got one shovel. Who's gonna dig?"

Brooks grinned at him. "You're the one holding it. Beauty before age. How's that line go? There are two kinds of people: guys with guns and guys who dig. And you dig."

"That's from *The Good, the Bad, and the Ugly*. But you ain't got no gun. How you gonna make me dig? You gonna write me an IOU that says you'll shoot me after I dig up the guns?"

Brooks grinned. "I can go back into the house and get my gun."

"You really are a pain in the ass," said Lefty.

He started digging. As he did he asked, "You like Tulsa?"

"It's not bad. I've seen better, I've seen worse."

"Have you been many places in your life?"

"Not really. I went to Vietnam."

"What was that like?"

"It sucked. It was the kind of place that makes you appreciate what we've got here."

"I didn't know you were in the Army."

"There's lots of things you don't know about me, kid. After being in the Army, getting paid to kill people made sense," said Brooks. "I guess you could say Uncle Sam made me the man I am today. The Vietnam War was kind of a gateway drug for me. And the pay as a hitter was a hell of a lot better than what I made working for Uncle Sam."

"So you killed people when you were in the Army?"

"I did a tour in Danang," said Brooks. "I hated it, but it's funny. I don't know why, and I guess this isn't uncommon, but despite my hating it, I look back at that time now as the best time of my life. I don't know why that is. Was it *really* the best time of my life? Probably not, but I look back on that fondly. I was so young then. I didn't know what the hell I was doing. I made a lot of friends over there, and I lost a lot of friends, too."

Lefty continued digging. He stopped for a second, leaning on the upright shovel handle, wiping his brow. "You wanna take over?"

"I got a bad back," said Brooks. "I'll tell you what: you keep digging and I'll make it up to you. I'll buy you dinner or something."

Lefty didn't really mind now that he was digging. So continued.

"So when we get to Detroit, how do we find Bruno De Lorenzo?" asked Brooks.

"He lives on the top floor of some hotel. I've gotta meet a guy when we get to Detroit. Some kind of broker, a middle man. He'll give me the details about the job, where to find De Lorenzo."

"I'm sure he's got security around him," observed Brooks.

"We can handle that. Does that concern you?"

"No, but that's more work. We get paid two million dollars to terminate De Lorenzo, but we don't make anything for having to kill those other poor bastards working for him."

"It's a hard knock life," said Lefty. "But still, it's two million dollars. I think we'll get by."

"But you have a contact there?"

"I've got a contact. He's the guy who'll pay us when the job is done."

"Good," said Brooks. "It would be a shit deal if we whacked De Lorenzo and then didn't get paid."

"We'll get paid."

"Another thing to think about," said Brooks. "A contract this big, there are gonna be other hitters showing up, trying to muscle in. There's gonna be competition. Hell, for all we know De Lorenzo's already dead."

"That's why we need to hurry up and get our asses to Detroit. Hopefully we don't have any more stops to make after we get Dixie." Lefty was about to make a smart-assed remark about Brooks bringing extra people along when the shovel struck something solid. He looked up at Brooks.

"There you go," said Brooks. "We'll get the guns up out of there, and then we're off, on our way to Oklahoma City."

FORTY-FIVE MINUTES later they were inside the Caddy, packed and ready to go.

"Brooks is coming with us?" asked Layla.

"Yes, Tator Tot."

"Where are we going?"

"The next place we're going is a place called Oklahoma City."

"Oklahoma City?" asked Layla. "What's in Oklahoma City?"

"Nothing worth a damn," answered Brooks.

"Then why are we going there?"

"We've got to meet another person," said Lefty.

Layla thought about this for a moment. "What's his name?"

"It's a lady this time," said Lefty.

"Dixie ain't no lady," interjected Brooks.

Layla asked, "Is she gonna come with us, too?"

"Probably," said Lefty. "We won't know for sure until we talk to her."

Layla nodded, taking it all in stride. "Daddy, can we listen to some music?"

"What do you wanna hear?"

"Sam Cooke."

"The little girl likes Sam Cooke?" asked Brooks. He hadn't spent much time around kids, not since he'd had his own, and even then he hadn't spent much time around them. He was surprised that a small child liked Sam Cooke, especially in this day and age of hippity-hoppity music and heavy metal.

"She's got good taste," said Lefty, retrieving the CD from the carrying case.

"She does," agreed Brooks.

"You like Sam Cooke?"

"Who doesn't like Sam Cooke? Now that I think about it, Spook was a big fan of his music, too."

"He was," said Lefty. "One of the man's only redeeming traits."

Lefty slid the CD into the stereo, pushed a couple of buttons, and Sam Cooke began singing "A Change Is Gonna Come."

"Nice choice," said Brooks.

Lefty looked at him. *You actually like this?*

"You sound surprised."

"I just thought..."

"I know what you thought," said Brooks. "This might

surprise you, kid, but I was in a parade with Dr. Martin Luther King once."

Lefty was visibly impressed. "No shit?"

"No shit," said Brooks. "Proudest day of my life."

"You're probably the only hitman who rode in a parade with Martin Luther King. How'd that happen?"

"I was working in a car dealership. They were thinking of having one of their cars in the parade, but none of those racist old bastards wanted to drive in it because they were opposed to what King was doing. So I said, 'I'll do it.' They said, 'You support him?' I said, 'Yes, I do.' They didn't like hearing that, but I wound up driving in the parade."

"That's terrific," said Lefty. "Did you get to meet the man?"

"No, I didn't. I wish I could tell you otherwise, but I can't. That'll forever be one of my biggest regrets."

Layla spoke up. "I wanna hear 'Having a Party.'"

"Is that your favorite Sam Cooke song?" asked Brooks.

"Yeah," said Layla. "That and 'Chain Gang.'"

"You don't like this one?"

"It's okay, I guess," said Layla. As smart as she was, she was still only seven, and the significance of the song was over her head.

"I'll turn it to that after this song is over," said Lefty.

The three of them drove for a few minutes, listening to Sam Cooke and staring out the window before Layla said, "I'm thirsty, Daddy."

"What do you wanna drink, Tator Tot?"

"I want a soda."

"What kind of soda do you want?"

The little girl considered this for a moment. After all, this was an extremely important decision. "Grape," she said.

"I want Grape. How about you? What kind of soda do you want, Daddy?"

"I think I'm in the mood for strawberry."

"Not me, I want grape." She paused for a moment before asking, "What kind of grape soda do you think is the best, Daddy?"

"I don't know. I like them all."

"Grape soda all tastes the same," said Brooks. "Like Kool-Aid."

Lefty, driving, turned to look at him. "The hell you say."

"What?"

"I'll give you that most grape sodas taste about the same, but you think Kool-Aid tastes the same as grape soda?"

"Yeah," said Brooks. "Everything grape tastes the same. It tastes like grape."

"They taste like the generic grape flavor to some degree, yeah, but there's a lot of wiggle room in there. They might have similar qualities, but they don't all taste the same."

"That's nonsense," said Brooks.

Lefty was becoming irritated for no good reason. "Does grape juice taste the same as grape soda?"

Brooks nodded. "Yeah, they're the same."

"No, they're not," said Lefty, irritation in his voice. "They absolutely are not the same. Have you ever had grape cough syrup?"

"Yeah."

"Do you think that tastes the same as grape soda, too?"

"Yeah," said Brooks. "It tastes like grape."

Lefty shook his head, staring at the highway ahead of them. "There's no talking sense to you. No wonder Dixie left you. I'll bet you were a huge pain in the ass to live with."

"I'm sure she wouldn't disagree."

"So why did she leave you anyway?" asked Lefty.

"Who said she left? How do you know it wasn't mutual?"

"Was it mutual?" asked Lefty, looking at him skeptically.

"Sure," said Brooks. "We mutually agreed that she didn't want to be married to me anymore."

Lefty laughed. "I can't wait to meet this woman."

"You'll probably get along great."

"Does she like black people?" asked Lefty.

"Of course," said Brooks. "Why do you ask?"

"Well, you said she didn't like Spook."

"That had nothing to do with his skin color. That was because he was an asshole."

Lefty nodded. "Yeah, he was an asshole for sure. So that still doesn't answer my question. Why did she leave?"

"She had her reasons."

"But you don't know what they were?"

"I have a few ideas."

"So, what are they?"

Brooks looked at him. "Can we just listen to Sam Cooke and ride along for a bit without talking?"

"Sure," said Lefty, and that's what they did.

SIX

THE ROAD TO OKLAHOMA CITY

THEY WERE SOMEWHERE between Tulsa and Oklahoma City when Lefty stopped at a tiny little gas station called Gas-N-Snaks to take a leak. After parking next to the building, he went in and pissed. When he walked out of the restroom, he was in the back of the gas station, getting his and Layla's bottles of soda, when he heard a ruckus in the front of the store. He turned and looked down the aisle. There was a middle-aged Hispanic man behind the counter, and there were a couple of ski-mask-wearing white guys aiming shotguns at him.

"Where's the goddamn surveilance camera?" one of the men screamed.

The clerk pointed up at a corner of the store above the soda fountain, where there was a camera mounted. "Up there," the clerk said nonchalantly. "But it doesn't work. It's been broken for a couple of years now. The boss keeps talking about getting it fixed, but he never does."

"You're lying!" said one of the robbers. "What kind of gas station doesn't have a surveillance camera?"

"A shitty one," said the clerk. "You don't know my boss.

He operates this place so poorly it's like he don't even give a shit. It's almost like this place was a front for the mob."

One of the robbers shoved his shotgun towards the clerk. "You'd better not be lying, Hector."

"That supposed to be a racial slur?" asked the clerk. "Pretty fuckin' weak, man. Hector? Your mama's name is Hector."

One of the robbers stepped towards the counter. "Just open the goddamn register and shut the fuck up."

The clerk looked at him. "You want the money?"

The two robbers looked at each other, and then the one who was doing all the talking said, "What the fuck else would we want, you dumb fucking beaner?"

The clerk didn't budge. "I'm not allowed to give you that money."

"*What?*" screamed the robber, infuriated. "What kind of bullshit is that?"

"My boss said if someone came in and stuck the place up, I wasn't supposed to give them the money."

The two robbers looked at each other again as if they were trying to figure out what to do next. One of them racked his shotgun.

"*That's bullshit!*" said the robber, flustered. "You'd better give me the goddamn money! *Do it now!*"

The clerk didn't move. "Really, I can't. If I give you the money, my boss'll fire me, and I need this job. I got child support to pay."

"Look, man, I'm not fucking around here," said the robber, almost pleading. "If you don't give me the money, I'll kill you. Simple as that. Would you rather be unemployed or dead?"

The clerk just stared at him, unimpressed. "I don't know what to tell you. I'm not giving you the money."

The robber moved forward. He tried to leap over the counter, but stumbled and fell behind it, hitting his head. *"Jesus Christ!"* he yelled in a whiny voice.

The clerk stood over him, laughing.

"You alright, Jerry?" asked the second robber.

Lefty couldn't see the fallen robber, still down behind the counter, but heard him say, "Don't say my fucking name, man. Now this guy knows me, you asshole." The robber stood up, raising his shotgun up under the clerk's chin. "Now I'm gonna have to waste him."

"Don't do that," said the other robber. "I don't wanna go back to the joint."

The robber just stood there staring at the clerk, only the shotgun between them. "I gotta do it, man. He'll tell the cops. You will, won't you, Hector?"

The clerk just stood there silently, not even arguing.

"Come on, man, we gotta go," said the second robber. "We're gonna get caught if we stick around here."

"We're not leaving without that money," said the first robber.

That was when Lefty came up behind the other robber, the .38 from his ankle up and out now. He put its barrel flush against the robber's head. "Don't move," he said. "It's too early in the day for me to have to kill you."

This caught the other robber's attention. He still had the shotgun up to the clerk's chin. Caught offguard he said, "Where the hell did you come from?"

Lefty grinned. "Don't do anything stupid, Jerry."

This made the robber angry. "I told you you shouldn't have said my name, Mark."

This made the clerk chuckle, despite the shotgun under his chin.

The robber looked at him angrily, readjusting the shotgun.

Lefty, still standing there with his .38 trained on the other robber, said, "Do you want me to shoot this guy for you?"

The clerk looked at him. "Are you talking to me?"

"Yeah."

The clerk looked at the guy holding the shotgun to his chin. "Sure, that would be great."

Lefty swiveled the .38 and fired on the robber, striking him in the cheek. The robber fell back hard against a rack of cigarettes and fell from sight. Lefty turned the .38 back to the other robber. "Your turn, pal."

"Please don't kill me," begged the robber.

Lefty fired a round into the back of his head, and the robber dropped. Lefty looked at the clerk, still standing there nonchalantly.

"Is the camera really broken?" asked Lefty.

The clerk nodded. "It is."

"You gonna tell the cops about this?"

"I didn't see the guy who shot these punks," said the clerk. "I think it was a skinny ginger-headed fuck on a motorcycle. He was wearing leather, like Freddie Mercury, and had sunglasses on." He thought for a moment. "And tattoos. Lots and lots of tattoos. One of 'em was a dragon that wrapped around his arm."

Lefty stuck the .38 into his pocket. "That's the guy I saw, too. I hope they catch him soon." He turned to leave, but stopped, grabbing a snack-sized bag of Cheetos from a rack. He looked around as he was leaving, but saw no one in the parking lot. He walked around the building to where the Caddy was parked. He climbed in and tossed the Cheetos back to Layla.

"Thanks, Daddy!" she chirped.

"No problem, Tator Tot."

"But what about my grape soda?"

"Sorry," said Lefty. "They didn't have any soda."

"No soda at all?" asked Layla.

"Surprisingly, no," lied Lefty.

Brooks gave him a skeptical look, trying to figure out what had happened. "Did I hear gunshots?"

"I don't think so."

"You were gone a long time, and you didn't get any soda. What gives?"

"The credit card machine was down. It took a minute."

Brooks knew there was more to the story but let it go. Lefty put the car into drive, and they were once again on their way to Oklahoma City to talk to Dixie.

ONCE THEY WERE in the city, they went to the address Brooks had written down. Lefty was surprised to discover that it was a church. It was was a quaint little white building with a sign out in front that announced it to be the First Church of the Holy Spirit. Lefty pulled the Caddy up in front of the place.

"Dixie lives in a church?" asked Lefty.

"No," said Brooks. "She's a minister."

"What the fuck? She's a minister?"

"That's exactly what I said when I found out about it. I guess she got some sort of license to be a minister online or something. I don't know how any of it works. She was always good at conning people. She's real smart, and she can talk her way in and out of just about any situation. I'm sure she's got these people believing she's the greatest thing since Moses parted the Red Sea."

"She's religious?"

"I've never known her to be," said Brooks. "The woman could curse and drink with the best of them. She said motherfucker more often than most sailors do. And she could drink just about any man under the table, myself included. And in bed..." Brooks stared off at nothing, imagining for a moment. He realized what he was doing and looked at Lefty. "She wasn't all that godly when I knew her. But things change. I haven't seen her in almost a decade."

"You didn't keep in touch?"

"Like I said, she's my *ex-wife*," said Brooks. "There's a reason for that."

Lefty nodded.

"Anyway, I'm sure she's had time to study up on the Bible or whatever. I guarantee you she knows her shit. Dixie's a woman who doesn't mess around. If she does something, she does it all the way. There's no half-assing with her."

"I've never heard of a hitter becoming a preacher before."

"Me neither," said Brooks. "But you know, I'm not surprised. This woman, she can do anything she wants. She's a total pain in the ass, but she can do just about anything she sets her mind to do."

Lefty grinned. Brooks saw this and asked, "What's so funny?"

"Between Dixie and my dad, you seem to be a magnet for people who are pains in the ass."

"While you're laughing," said Brooks, "let's not forget about you."

Lefty feigned offense. "Are you saying I'm a pain in the ass?"

"The rotten apple didn't fall far from the tree."

Lefty chuckled.

"I'll be right back," said Brooks.

"Do you have a plan? Or are you just gonna walk into the church and tell her to come with us? Are you even sure she's gonna wanna do this?"

Brooks smiled. "I know this woman. Trust me, she'll come to Detroit."

Brooks climbed out of the car and walked into the church. It being a weekday, middle of the day, the lobby was as empty as Al Capone's vault. He looked around. He saw an open office door. He peered in and saw a fat black man sitting in there staring at a computer screen.

"Excuse me," said Brooks.

The man looked up. "Can I help you?"

"I'm looking for Dixie Jackson. Do you know where I might find her?"

The man sat up a bit. "She called a little while ago. She's downtown. There's a guy out on a ledge, threatening to jump. He wanted to talk to someone about God, so they called Dixie." The man thought about it for a moment. "You're a cop, aren't you? You probably already knew about that."

Brooks didn't hesitate. "Yeah, I'm a cop. You got me. I guess it's kind of obvious, huh?"

The man grinned. "I can usually tell."

"Right," said Brooks.

"What's your name, officer?"

"Uh, Detective..." Brooks looked around, desperately searching for a name. His eyes fell upon a painting of the crucifixion. "My name is Christ."

The man cocked his head and made a funny face. "Your name is Detective *Christ*?"

"I know," said Brooks. "Trust me, I know. You try

growing up with a name like that and see how you get along."

"I'll bet the kids made fun of you in school."

"All the time," said Brooks. "Every single day. The neighborhood kids, they'd try to crucify me. They made a cross, tried to nail me to it."

"How'd that go?"

"I learned how to fight," said Brooks. "I beat the living shit out of every one of those little fuckers."

The man looked shocked and offended. He cleared his throat, making a show out of not saying anything.

"So yeah, I'm a cop. Detective Christ."

The man sat there for a moment, staring at him, thinking about it. "Hold up. If you're a cop, why are you here? You already know where she's at, right?"

"Must have been a mix-up down at the station. I thought I was supposed to come and get her, take her up there. I didn't realize she was already there...at...the, uh, building." Brooks stared at the man. "What's the name of that building again?"

The man looked suspicious, but said, "Chase Tower."

"Right," said Brooks. He turned to leave, but stopped and turned back to the man. "And where's that located again?"

BROOKS WAS surprised how easily he'd gained access to the 12th floor, where Dixie and the would-be jumper were. All he'd said was that he was from the church (luckily they didn't ask the name of the church, because he couldn't have remembered it to save his life) and had come to assist her. Easy peezy, they let him walk right in. There were some cops congregated by the office door (and there were a ton of cops and firemen down on the street in case the man jumped). The office itself was empty. Brooks found Dixie standing just outside the open window, talking to a man who was standing out there on the ledge a few steps down. As he approached the window, Brooks could hear Dixie's familiar voice telling the man about Christ's infinite love.

Brooks stuck his head outside the window. Dixie didn't see him at first. Brooks waited until she was done talking before saying, "Hello, Dixie." She turned and looked at him, more than a little stunned.

"Well, hell, I guess we got us a party here," she said. "What in God's name are you doing here?"

Brooks smirked. "I came to join this guy. I'm gonna jump, too."

Brooks looked around Dixie at the confused man, who was trying to figure out what was going on.

"You should do it then," said Dixie. "I won't stop you. You'd be doing us all a favor, Brooks."

"I see you're still pissed at me, but then you usually were."

"Don't give me that shit, Brooks Barker. You're not innocent. You were never innocent. I gave you hell, but you deserved every bit of it. Truth be told, you probably deserved more than I ever gave you."

The would-be jumper watched all this.

Brooks looked over at him and offered a half-hearted wave. "I'm Brooks."

The man looked unsure. He kind of stuttered out, "Dave."

"Good to meet you, Dave."

Dixie looked at him. "This worthless sonofabitch is my ex-husband. He's a lying, no good piece of shit. Isn't that right, Brooks?"

Dave gave Brooks a look as if to say he was sorry for what he was enduring.

"I wasn't always the best husband," said Brooks.

"You think?" asked Dixie. "You slept with my daughter!" She was really pissed now. *"My daughter, asshole!"*

Brooks felt bad, knowing he'd done a bad thing. "Do you guys talk?" asked Brooks.

"Who?" asked Dixie.

"You and your daughter."

"As a matter of fact, Brooks, yes, we do talk. But that's none of your business."

"She doing okay?"

"She's doing fine, living in Portland with her new husband."

"Tell her hello for me," said Brooks.

Dixie looked at him, her expression threatening bodily harm. "Why are you here, Brooks? What do you want? I haven't heard from you in nine years and now, suddenly, you show up out of the blue. Obviously you want something. What is it?"

"I got a job to offer you."

She paused, staring at him for a beat. "What kind of job?"

"The normal kind," said Brooks. "The kind we always did."

"I thought you were through with all that."

"So did I," said Brooks. "Remember Spook?"

"Of course I remember Spook." She turned and looked at Dave. "Spook was even worse than this piece of shit. And that's saying a whole lot."

"Spook's dead now."

Brooks thought Dixie might be moved by this, but she wasn't. "And?"

"His son came to see me."

"Yeah? What about?"

"He's a hitter now, like Spook was. He told me about a job."

"Why's he telling you?"

"He wants me to help him," said Brooks. "His daddy told him if he ever needed help, he should look me up. So he did."

"So what's this got to do with me?"

Brooks looked at her. "This is a special job."

She was paying attention now. "What's so special about it?"

"The contract is for two million dollars."

"Two million dollars? For one guy?"

"One guy," said Brooks. He made a show of looking over at Dave in an effort to remind Dixie he was still over there.

"Don't worry about him," she said dismissively. "What do you want with me?"

"I want your help."

She looked at him with suspicion. "Why?"

"You're the best hitter I know," said Brooks. "And I owe you."

She stood there on the ledge for a moment in silence, looking down at the street below, mulling it over. "You do owe me. You owe me *a lot*."

"You think $666,000 will cover it?"

"Not even close," she said. "But it's a start."

Brooks smiled, slightly relieved.

"What about me?" asked Dave.

Brooks looked at him. "Why do you wanna jump, Dave? What's the problem?"

"It's my old lady," said Dave.

"She leave?"

"Yeah, and she took my kid."

"Sucks about the kid. But you're gonna find that you're better off without the wife. I guarantee it. It may not seem like it now, but one of these days you're gonna wake up and realize that was the best thing that ever happened to you."

Dixie gave him a disapproving look. "That how you feel, Brooks? You think my leaving was the best thing that ever happened to you?"

"In some ways," admitted Brooks, nodding. "It's nice to not have to argue all the time."

"I'm sure you're just out there sleeping with anything that'll have you."

Brooks laughed. "You'd be surprised. I haven't had sex in a long time now. Years."

"You know they got pills for that, right?"

"That ain't the problem. I'm an old man now. Girls aren't exactly lining up to sleep with an old codger like me."

"There's your problem. You're looking for *girls*. You need to look for a woman."

"Sometimes I go to the titty bar," said Brooks.

"You take the strippers home?"

"I have, but it's been a long time."

Dixie looked at him. "Why's that?"

"It's so impersonal," said Brooks. "It ain't like it was with you."

"Now you miss me?" she asked. "Maybe you should have tried not screwing my daughter."

Brooks looked over at Dave. "She wasn't my daughter. She was from another marriage."

"What the hell?" asked Dixie.

"I didn't want him to think I had sex with my own daughter."

"Why do you care what he thinks?"

"That wouldn't be right."

"Having sex with my daughter wasn't right either, Brooks."

He nodded. "Okay, you got me there."

"So where's this job?"

"It's in Detroit."

"Detroit?" she asked. "No wonder it pays two million. No one would go there otherwise. Detroit is all kinds of nasty. It's a goddamn shithole."

"Tell me about it," said Brooks. "But that's where it is."

Dixie sat down in the window, her legs dangling off the ledge. She looked at Brooks. "You got a cigarette?"

"I quit five years ago."

"Figures," said Dixie. She looked over at Dave. "How about you? You smoke?"

Dave nodded that he did. He reached into his pocket and produced a pack of Winstons. He handed the pack and a lighter over to Dixie. She took a cigarette out and held it up, lighting it. She looked over at Dave. "So what's up, Dave? Are you gonna jump today or what? What's the deal here?"

"I don't know."

"Jumping seems like a shit deal," said Brooks. "Think about your kid. What you got? A daughter?"

"No," said Dave. "I got a son. He's twelve."

"Do you remember when you were twelve, Dave?"

Dave nodded. "Sure."

"What would your life have been like if your father had killed himself when you were twelve?" asked Brooks.

Dave said, "My dad died when I was a baby."

"Let me rephrase that then. How did you like growing up without a father?"

Dave was considering this.

97

"You didn't like it, did you?" asked Dixie, taking a drag.

"No, I guess I didn't."

"You like your kid?" asked Brooks.

"Yeah, I do," said Dave. "And he likes me."

"Well shit," said Brooks. "That's half the battle right there."

"Lots of kids don't like their parents," added Dixie.

Dave nodded. "I didn't like my mom."

"But I'll bet you still wanted her alive," said Brooks. "And you didn't even like her. Just think about how your son, who actually likes you, would feel if you were gone."

Dave was silent, an expression of uncertainty on his face.

"Goddammit, Dave," said Dixie. "Let's cut through the bullshit. Are you gonna jump or what?"

"I don't know."

"The clock is ticking, tick fucking tock, Dave," said Dixie. "It's time to shit or get off the pot."

Dave's expression was priceless. He didn't know how to react.

Dixie flicked the cigarette down towards the street below. "Fuck this," said, rising to her feet. "I'm leaving. You do what you want, Dave. Jump or don't jump, it's up to you."

And she left, Brooks following her.

Dave stood there, unsure what was happening. He looked to the sky and he started to cry.

AFTER LEAVING CHASE TOWER, everyone was in the Cadillac. The two males were in the front, and the two women were in back. Lefty turned on the stereo and Marvin Gaye was there with them, singing "Trouble Man."

Dixie looked at Layla, taking a break from her tablet. "What's your name, sweetheart?"

"My name is Layla. What's yours?"

"I'm Dixie.

Layla smiled big. "Pleased to meet you."

"How old are you?"

"I'm seven. How old are you?"

Dixie looked startled for a moment. Before she could say anything, Brooks spoke up. "She's old as the hills."

"What does that mean?" asked Layla.

"It means she's really old," said Brooks.

Dixie said, "Don't you mind him, Layla. He's just a grumpy old man."

Layla nodded. "I know."

This response caused everyone in the car to chuckle.

"So where do you live, Dixie?" asked Lefty. "I assume you want to go there and get some clothes together?"

"That would be helpful. Take a right up here at the corner." She looked at Brooks. "So tell me about this job."

"Let's not forget, Layla is in the car with us," reminded Lefty.

Dixie snapped, "Says the guy who brought the little girl in the first place."

Brooks grinned. "I think she likes you already, Lefty."

"I've got nothing against you," she said. "But if you're anything like your daddy..."

Lefty looked at her in the rear-view mirror. "I assure you I'm not."

"Okay, good. Then we'll get along just fine."

"We can still talk about the job," said Dixie. "We can just talk about it discreetly."

Layla spoke up. "I know what discreetly means."

Dixie looked at her. Brooks said, "She's a smart kid."

"So I see," said Dixie. "So tell me more."

"It's two million," said Lefty.

"For one person," Dixie said.

"One guy."

"Who the hell is this guy we're, uh, going to see?"

Brooks said, "His last name is De Lorenzo if that tells you anything."

An expression of realization appeared on Dixie's face. "The Don?"

"Not Don Antonio," said Lefty. "It's his son, Bruno."

Dixie nodded, taking it in. "And who, uh, who's behind this thing?"

"No one knows," said Lefty.

"Then how do we get the money?"

"There's a guy in Detroit," said Lefty. "A lawyer. A middle man. I'm supposed to meet with him to get the details. He's the same guy who pays the money."

"Trouble Man" came to its conclusion and Lefty pushed the repeat button. The song started up again.

"That's a lot of money," said Dixie.

"Sure is," said Brooks.

"Daddy," said Layla.

"Yes, Tator Tot?"

"How much is two million?"

"It's a big number."

"How big?"

"Real big."

This didn't satisfy her. "How many zeros are in a million?"

Lefty started to think about it, but Dixie blurted, "Six."

"So two million has twelve zeros?" asked Layla.

"No, sweetheart," said Dixie. "It still has six."

Layla frowned. "I don't get it."

"Sometimes life is confusing," said Brooks.

Dixie made a face and looked at the little girl. "You want confusing, you should try being married to a jackass for twenty years."

Layla frowned, not understanding.

Brooks said, "Don't listen to her. She's a grumpy old hag."

Layla nodded again. "I know."

Dixie told Lefty where and when to turn, and eventually they were in front of the Crescent apartment building. "This is your place?" asked Lefty.

"This is where the magic happens," she said.

Brooks said, "It looks like a shithole."

"Kiss my ass, old man."

Layla frowned again. "She said a bad word, Daddy."

"It's okay," said Lefty. "Sometimes old people say bad things."

Layla nodded. "I know."

THE FOUR OF them got on the road to Detroit around six. It was a fifteen-hour drive, so they decided to stop somewhere for the night. Lefty did all the driving, and they drove until just after midnight. When they pulled into the archaic little relic of a motel, both Dixie and Layla were asleep in the back.

Lefty and Brooks went into the office and secured adjoining rooms, each one with two beds. Brooks insisted on paying for both rooms, telling Lefty, "Don't worry about it. It's on me. But Dixie? She can pay me back." They left wake-up calls for six in the morning.

"If we get on the road by seven, we should be in Detroit before evening," said Lefty. They woke up the women and carried the bags to the rooms. Once Lefty and Layla were in their beds in the dark, Layla said, "What about my bedtime story?"

Lefty sighed. He had forgotten about their usual bedtime story, assuming it was late enough he wouldn't have to tell one. He felt tired and didn't want to come up with a story.

"What if I tell you a story?" asked Layla. "Would that be okay?"

Lefty said sure. He barely managed to stay awake, but listened to Layla concoct a story she called "The Clown of Death." The story was about an evil clown who ate people's heads, ending with the gruesome death of the protagonist. After the story was finished, Lefty and Layla went to sleep.

SEVEN
THE CHAMPAGNE ROOM

THE NEXT MORNING LEFTY, Brooks, and Layla walked over to the McDonalds across the street to get breakfast. Dixie didn't come, citing an intense dislike for McDonalds. The place was mostly full, as was any McDonalds at almost any time anywhere in this part of the country, where the restaurant was treated with an unrivaled reverence, an indicator as to why obesity was rampant in the fly-over states.

As the three of them sat at a table, Lefty and Layla on one side, Brooks on the other, they ate their Sausage McMuffins and conversed.

"I still can't believe I'm talking to Spook Collins' boy," said Brooks.

Lefty nodded. "Funky fresh, in the flesh."

"What does your mama say about Spook these days?"

"We don't talk about my dad."

"Never?"

"Never ever."

"They broke up on bad terms, I guess?"

"If you call him beating the shit out of her and breaking

her collar bone and a couple of her ribs bad terms, then yeah, they broke up on bad terms."

"Goddamn Spook," said Brooks. "He always was a real sweetheart."

"But you still liked him?"

"Sure, but that don't mean I approve of beating on women, because I don't. I don't think it's right. I've heard guys argue that women deserve to be treated as equals to men, but it's funny 'cause those same men only seem to say that when it comes to women getting their asses kicked. They don't seem to feel that way when it comes to anything that might actually be good for the woman."

Layla looked up from her breakfast. "What are you talking about, Daddy?"

Lefty looked at Brooks, a wary expression on his face. "Don't worry about it, Tator Tot," he said. "This is grown-up talk."

"Why?"

"Some things are just grown-up conversations."

She pressed. "But why?"

Lefty looked at Brooks, amused by Layla's questioning.

Lefty decided to let her in on it. "We were talking about when boys hit girls. You know that's bad, right?"

"Of course. Billy Cartright hit my friend Maddie on the playground one day. He pulled back his arm and punched her right in the tummy."

"That's not good," said Lefty. "Did Billy get in trouble?"

"No, but Maddie punched him in the Adam's Apple and kicked him in the nuts."

Lefty and Brooks both chuckled.

"What did he do after that?" asked Lefty.

Layla beamed. "He fell on the ground and cried. He

peed his pants, too. After that, everyone at school started calling him Billy Pee Pants."

"Maddie sounds pretty tough," said Brooks.

Layla said excitedly, "She is. She can fight like a ninja."

"Layla here can fight pretty good, too," said Lefty. "She's in Ju Kempo."

"What's Ju Kempo?" asked Brooks.

"It's like Karate," said Layla. "Only different."

"It's a different martial art," explained Lefty.

"Are you a black belt?" asked Brooks.

"Not yet," said Layla, now deathly serious. "Maybe in a year or so."

Lefty smiled. "It's probably gonna take a little bit longer than a year, Tator Tot."

Layla ignored this, still looking at Brooks. "I'm a yellow belt."

"Oh yeah?" asked Brooks. "Is that pretty good?"

"It's my second belt," she said. "The first one was white."

"How long have you been in Ju Klemto?" asked Brooks.

"Ju Kempo," she corrected. "It's been a long time."

"About a year," said Lefty, smiling. He looked down at Layla's decimated Sausage McMuffin, lying there in pieces. "Why are you taking all your food apart?"

"I like to eat the muffin and the sausage at different times. Then it's like I have more food. And I eat the cheese by itself, too. I just peel it off the sausage and eat it."

"That's a good way to do it, I guess," said Brooks.

"Layla wouldn't even eat meat until about a year ago," said Lefty.

Brooks looked at the little girl. "So what did you eat?"

"Pizza," said Layla, nibbling on the sausage-less muffin.

Lefty looked at Brooks. "I need to ask you for a favor."

"Another one?"

"I'm serious," said Lefty.

"I may not do it, but you can ask."

"I'm supposed to meet that lawyer, the broker. But Layla can't go with me. Could you and Dixie watch her for a little bit while I'm gone?"

Brooks looked at the little girl, unsure.

It was just after eleven when Lefty walked into the strip club. Stepping out of the bright sunlight into this darkest of dark places gave him the sense he was walking into a vampire's lair. "Welcome to Teaser's," said the burly door man, sitting on a stool by the entrance.

Lefty looked around. At this time of day Teaser's was the refuge of the lowliest of the lowly and the loneliest of the lonely. There were a couple of sleazy-looking guys situated around the bar and the stage, probably capping off a long night rather than starting a new day. The place reeked of cigarette smoke and cheap perfume. There was some kind of awful dance music pulsating from the overhead speakers. There was a solitary stripper onstage, who looked like she was forty-five if she was a day.

The bouncer took Lefty's twelve bucks and let him in. "You get two drinks with that," he informed him.

Lefty walked inside and approached the bartender. "Excuse me."

The bartender turned and looked at him.

"I'm looking for a lawyer, goes by the name of Frankie Gio."

The bartender simultaneously nodded and grinned. He pointed over to some doors in the distance. "Second door is his," the bartender said. "If you get to the john, you've gone too far."

Lefty thanked him and walked towards the office. The door was closed. He now saw there was a clumsily-scrawled sign taped to it. It had Gio's name written on it. Lefty knocked.

"Come in," came a voice from inside.

He opened the door and found a sleazy-looking heavyset goomba with leathery skin, approximately fifty, sitting at a desk watching porn on his PC. He looked up, a cigarette dangling from his bottom lip. "What can I do you for?"

"I'm supposed to give you a password," said Lefty.

This got Gio's attention. "What's the password?"

"Avocado."

Gio lit up, nodding. "Right, avo-fuckin'-cado."

"I need details about the contract."

"I'll give you what I can," said Gio. He stood up, wiping food crumbs off his t-shirt/sports coat combo. He reached out a hand for him to shake. Lefty didn't want to shake it, but he did, thankful to find it neither sweaty nor slick from lotion. When they unlocked hands, Gio came around the desk and walked to the door. "Follow me," he said. "We'll go somewhere we can talk."

This surprised Lefty as he would have thought Gio's office a sufficient locale for their discussion. A few steps outside, Gio turned back to him. "Are you straight?"

"What do you mean?"

Gio rolled his eyes. "Do you like pussy?"

Lefty grinned. "Who doesn't?"

"Right," said Gio, nodding. "Even women like pussy. At least the good ones anyway." Gio walked over to the bartender and said something, but Lefty couldn't make it out. Gio and the bartender then parted ways. The bartender scurried off, and Gio came back over to where Lefty was standing.

"Come on," said Gio, leading him. "We can talk in here."

Gio led him to a door labeled the Champagne Room. Lefty wondered what all this was about, but he wasn't about to turn down the charms of a shapely young woman if they were offered to him. They entered the Champagne Room and there were two chairs in the center of the room and a couch along the back wall. Gio motioned towards the chairs. "Have a seat."

Lefty sat down.

"Where you from?"

"Does it matter?" asked Lefty.

"Not particularly," said Gio, still standing there, removing a pack of smokes from inside his sports coat. "You mind if I smoke?"

Lefty shrugged. "It's your place."

"I don't own it or anything. I just got an office here."

"I've never seen a lawyer with an office inside a strip club before."

Gio grinned. "What can I say? I'm one of a kind." Gio started to say something else, but the door opened. Two young strippers strode in, wearing only bottoms and heels, their tits on full display.

Gio put his hand on one of the girls' arm, leading her in. "Ladies," he said. "Come on in. I want you to meet my friend here." He looked at Lefty, realizing he still didn't know his name.

"Call me Lefty," he said. The girls both smiled, their eyes sizing him up. They giggled. One of them, a sexy

Latina with long black hair, climbed on Lefty's lap, strad-dling him. Lefty looked at Gio. "This one's forward."

"That's the best way for a broad to be," said Gio, sitting down in the chair beside him. "Who's got time to fuck around, am I right? I figure it's better if they just get in there and do the thing, you know?"

Lefty looked up at the girl sitting on his lap, her medium-sized tits in his face. She was beautiful. He was certain she had broken a heart or two before, back when she was Maria or whomever she was out in the real world. "What's your name?" he asked.

"Candi," she purred.

"Candi? Why does that sound like a bullshit stripper name to me? I've never seen a Hispanic girl named Candi before."

Candi grinned. "Judging by how hard your dick is right now, I don't think you really care too much what my name is."

"Just making conversation," said Lefty.

The other girl was now straddling Gio, who looked completely disinterested, causing Lefty to wonder how many lap dances the man received.

"Tell me about the mark," said Lefty, still looking at Candi. She was trying to look sexy, feigning interest. Lefty was pretty sure he could fall in love with this girl if he let himself. So he vowed he that wouldn't, no matter what his dick had to say about the matter.

"I'm sure you know who the mark is," said Gio.

"I do. Real colorful character. But who's putting up the money?"

Gio looked past the silicone breasts in his face, making eye contact with Lefty. "I am."

"Right, but who's behind you?"

"That's one of those need-to-know kind of things."

"And?"

Gio grinned big. "You don't need to know."

Lefty nodded, looking back at Candi, grinding on his dick. "You like that?" she asked. He nodded, then turned back to Gio. "So nobody knows who's behind this thing?"

"Well, I do," said Gio. "But that's it. And maybe Bruno De Lorenzo. *Maybe*. But that guy's pissed off enough people he might not know for sure either."

Lefty said, "That's what I hear. The guy is legendary for his bad behavior."

Gio nodded, smirking. "He'd done a couple things."

"So answer me this: what's to stop Bruno De Lorenzo from having his goons come down here and stick a gun in your mouth and force you to tell him who's behind the contract?"

"This your first time in Detroit?"

"Yeah," said Lefty. "Why?"

"That's not how we do it here. I work for everyone, across the board. There's an agreement, and that agreement says that nobody touches me. It's been this way for a long time, and nobody crosses those lines."

"I would think the Don would be interested in finding out who's behind this."

Gio nodded. "He probably is, but again, there's an agreement here that nobody comes after me. I'm just the middle man. I work for all these guys. I ain't never fucked with nobody, nobody fucks with me."

"What about me?" asked the stripper on Gio's lap.

Gio grinned big. "You got me, kiddo. I fuck with you, and I fuck with you good, huh?"

She grinned and looked at Lefty. "You do alright."

Gio pretended to be offended. "That's fucked up, Angie. You're hurting my feelings."

Angie just giggled again. "How about I kiss you and make it better?"

Gio looked at her. "You think your kisses are gonna make me feel better?"

"I suppose it depends on where I kiss you," she said.

"So where's Bruno De Lorenzo stay?" interrupted Lefty. "I heard he lives in a big hotel somewhere."

"He lives on the top floor of the Belmont," said Gio. "Penthouse."

"Lots of security?"

"Normally just a few guys, but with this contract on his head, there's likely to be more."

"How many guys are on the job?" asked Lefty. "How many hitters have you spoken to so far?"

"I really can't say," said Gio. "But there are others."

Candi, riding on Lefty's dick, said, "You guys just gonna talk all night, or you gonna fuck us?"

"Dirty mouth on this one," said Lefty.

"Dirtier than you might think."

Gio looked to Lefty to see what he was gonna to do.

"That sounds like a threat," said Lefty.

Candi bit her bottom lip seductively. "More like a promise." She reached back and fondled his balls.

"Don't worry," said Lefty. "I'll fuck you. Make no bones about it, that's gonna happen. But right now we're talking business."

"So what's your point?" asked Candi.

"Let the grown folks talk, sweetheart," said Gio.

"Then?" asked Angie.

"Then we're gonna do some blow."

"Off our tits?"

Gio nodded. "Sure. Off your tits and asses."

"Then what?"

"Then I'm gonna screw the taste out of that dirty mouth of yours," said Lefty.

"Ooh," purred Candi. "Sounds yummy."

"You don't know the half of it."

She looked at Lefty. "You wanna do some blow?"

"Does a bear shit in the woods?"

Angie inquired, "Is this a domesticated bear?"

"Nah, just a regular old black bear living up on Shit Mountain."

"What's that supposed to mean?"

"It means let's do some blow."

"How do we know you're not a cop?"

"Do I look like a cop?" asked Lefty, offended.

"Girls," said Gio. "Do I ever come back here with cops?"

The girls looked at each other. "Sometimes," said Candi.

Gio nodded. "Got me there. Sometimes. But not today."

Lefty looked at Candi, at big brown eyes he could get lost in. "What's your story, Candi? How'd you end up here?"

Candi shrugged. "Dumb luck, I guess."

"No, really. I'm curious."

"I'm tryin' to pay my way through college."

"That's what they all say."

"Well, fuck them. I'm actually going to college."

"What's your major?"

"What do you care?"

"How am I supposed to bang you if I don't know your background?"

Candi smiled. "Accounting."

"You're an accounting major? Where you from, Candi?"

"Texas."

"You from Dallas?"

"Believe it or not, we've got other shit in Texas besides Dallas. I'm from a teeny-tiny little small town in the middle of nowhere. You wouldn't know it."

"Try me."

"Anderson," she said.

Lefty laughed. "You're right. I don't know it."

"You wouldn't," said Candi. "You could have actually driven through it and you probably still wouldn't know it. It's pretty nondescript. It's just one of those small towns, like a million other podunk towns in the South."

"So you came to Detroit?"

Candi nodded. "I did." She looked at Gio. "Can I have a smoke?"

"Sure," said Gio. "But when you end up with cancer, don't blame me."

Gio pulled out the pack, removed a single cigarette, and handed it to Candi, along with the lighter. She looked at Lefty as she placed the cigarette to her lips. "You care if I smoke?"

"It's a free country."

Candi looked at him like he was stupid. "You're a black man. You know better than that." She lit the cigarette, getting it going. She handed the lighter back to Gio.

"Your family know you strip for a living?" asked Lefty.

"Of course not."

"What do you think you do?"

"They think I sell furniture at this big warehouse store."

Gio laughed. "Why on earth would they think that?"

"I used to work there," said Candi. "I just never told 'em I got fired."

"What made you want to be an accountant?"

"The money. Accountants make good money."

"I'll bet a pretty girl like you makes good money here."

"I do, but there's no future in it."

"You don't like your job?"

Candi looked at him, trying to understand. "What's to like?"

"You get healthcare benefits?"

Both strippers laughed at this.

"Christ no," said Candi.

"And you hook also?"

"Not really."

"What does that mean?"

"I occasionally screw guys for money, sure, but it's only the guys I wanna screw." She looked over at Gio. "Well, and Gio. I screw him, too." They all laughed at this. "But seriously," she said. "It's not like I'm a real hooker, where I'm dependent on the money and I gotta screw every sleazeball who walks through the door."

Lefty started to say something else, but Candi put her finger over his mouth. "Why don't we stop talking now?"

"Or what?"

"Or I'll stop riding your dick."

"Okay, you win."

Candi intently gazed down at Lefty. "Do you think I'm sexy, baby?"

"Can't you feel my dick?" he asked. "It's harder than Chinese arithmetic."

Candi reached back and caressed his shaft. "That's for me?"

"Every inch of it," said Lefty.

"Awwww," she said, trying to sound cute. "You're so sweet."

"I guess that didn't sound so cute coming out of my mouth."

Candi stuck her finger in his mouth. "Wanna hear how cute I can sound coming *in* your mouth?"

LEFTY WAS DRIVING BACK from the strip club when he spotted a coney dog restaurant with a drive-thru. While having sex with Candi he'd worked up an appetite, so he pulled in. Being the single dad of a seven-year-old, sexual encounters were few and far between for him. Candi had served as an adequate reminder of the things in life he was missing. But between raising Layla and killing people, there just wasn't time to go out and meet women. It took far too long to get to know them and share intimacies and do and say all the things it required to get a non-professional girl into bed. And even then, Lefty didn't want to risk being discovered as the professional killer he was. So for now it would just remain he and Layla, a house of two.

As Lefty sat idling in the drive-thru, waiting his turn and listening to the O'Jays, he thought about the Bruno De Lorenzo contract. Sitting there, he raised his cell phone and looked up the Belmont Hotel to get an idea where De Lorenzo was staying. There was a Wikipedia entry for the hotel. Lefty scanned the article, reading about the hotel's long history of Mafia activity. It didn't really tell him anything that would be of use.

When Lefty finally edged up to the window, he paid for the sack of dogs he'd ordered. The young guy at the window handed him the sack and his large Sprite. He sat the bag on the seat beside him, placed the cup in the cup holder, and pulled out of the drive-thru. He was driving along, tapping his fingers on the steering wheel, lost in thought, when he came to Broadway. Remembering that the Belmont was located on Broadway, he decided to drive past the hotel to get a look at the place before going back to the motel.

Being the horrible navigator that he was, Lefty got turned around a couple of times before he located the hotel, but at long last he found it. It was a big tall building, jutting up towards the sky. Despite having been built in the 1920s, it didn't look particularly archaic. Lefty parked the Caddy on the side of the street, deciding to sit there and watch the building for a few minutes as he scarfed down his food.

As he was sitting there eating, Lefty saw a bald-headed black man parked in a black Escalade on the other side of the street, also watching the hotel. Lefty stared for a moment, recognizing him. It was Orlando Williams, a contract hitter out of Los Angeles. The bosses in the Midwest sometimes called Orlando for special jobs, as he was considered the absolute best in the business. Lefty watched Orlando, but Orlando never noticed him. They had met once in passing, but there was no reason Orlando should remember him. Lefty was probably too far down the food chain for Orlando to bother remembering, even if they were basically the only two black hitters the Mafia employed.

But Lefty was pretty sure he would make his mark on Orlando's life today. It didn't take a rocket scientist to figure out why Orlando was here, and Lefty wasn't about to lose out on his big payday. So, he concluded, he would have to kill Orlando Williams.

EIGHT
A WORTHY ADVERSARY

LEFTY SAT THERE WATCHING the guy for awhile, but Orlando Williams didn't seem to notice. Orlando Williams was Lefty's hero. He was the first black hitman the Mafia had ever utilized, so he was a fucking legend. Before Orlando had paved the way, Lefty's father had been working for black gangsters in Chicago. It was only because of Orlando's proven efficiency that Spook was eventually hired by the mob. Since then there had only one other black hitter, and that was Lefty.

Orlando was a curious case, to be sure. The Mafioso would talk about him with reverence, in a way that these Italian "men of honor" never spoke of any other black man. They called him the Professor, because, as the story went, Orlando Williams had once been a UCLA professor by day and a hitter by night. But none of that was what made him the stuff of legend. It wasn't even the remarkable number of hits he'd pulled off over the years.

No, Orlando Williams had done something no one else had ever done before and certainly no one else—especially a black man—would have been allowed to survive having done. Orlando Williams single-handedly wiped out an entire Mafia family in Los Angeles. He then slipped into the wind for a bit, hiding out somewhere; some people said the Caribbean, others said France. Then, eventually, he turned up stateside, reaching out to the Commission to plead his case. The Commission had experienced some real problems with the Los Angeles crew and had been secretly pleased with Orlando's killing them, saving them the hassle of doing it themselves. So, despite the objections of a few of the older mustache Petes, Orlando Williams had been allowed back into the fold.

Lefty watched Orlando pull away from the curb. Lefty followed, staying a ways behind so the older hitman wouldn't know he was being followed. The Ojays were now singing "For the Love of Money" on Lefty's stereo, perfectly summing up the situation Lefty was in. Here he was, about to murder his hero, and it was all because of money. As Lefty considered this, still following the Escalade, he thought about the old saying about money being the root of all evil. He didn't necessarily believe in good or evil, but he definitely agreed that money was the root of a lot of really fucked up shit.

Lefty followed Orlando as he cruised through Detroit, making occasional turns here and there. Finally Orlando pulled into the parking lot of another high-rise hotel. This one was called the Dumont. Lefty figured this was where Orlando was staying. As Orlando settled into a parking spot, Lefty drove around the block so he wouldn't be seen. When he came back around to the parking lot from its side, he could see Orlando walking towards the building. Lefty parked alongside the curb on the outside of the lot. He climbed out of the car, grabbing his silenced Glock 23 from the floor, sliding it into the shoulder holster in his jacket. He began making his way towards the building, watching Orlando enter. Lefty was still a fair distance behind, so he broke into a sprint. After all, he didn't want to lose the guy after coming this far.

When Lefty got to the front door, he stepped inside. There was a large lobby area and a desk with a couple of fat women sitting behind it. He smiled at them, nodding, trying to look like he belonged here and knew exactly where he was going. It worked, and neither of them paid him any mind. Orlando was nowhere in sight. When Lefty walked around the corner into the larger, more fully-exposed part of the lobby, he saw the elevator doors closing with Orlando standing alone inside. Lefty bolted towards the closing doors. In the briefest of seconds, the two mens' eyes locked, and Lefty blurted, *"Hold that door!"* Just before the doors would have clapped shut, Orlando reached his arm through, causing them to reopen. Lefty lurched forward, now doing a brisk walk, and got in the elevator.

Christ, this was gonna be awkward.

Orlando smiled nonchalantly. "How's it going?"

"Not bad. You?"

"I suppose I could complain, but no one would listen," said Orlando, grinning. He reached out, his hand hovering over the buttons. "What floor you going to?" Lefty saw that Orlando had hit the button for floor sixteen, so he answered, "Floor sixteen please." Orlando pulled his hand back, lowering it beside him. Lefty was prepared to reach for his Glock if things went sideways. But Orlando was unaffected by his coincidentally going to the same floor. "Me too," said Orlando.

"What?"

"Floor sixteen. We're going to the same floor."

Lefty smiled and nodded, pretending to learn this for

the first time. "I guess they're sticking all the black folks on the same floor."

Orlando laughed. "There goes the neighborhood."

As they rode without speaking, the elevator speakers gently played "The Girl from Ipanema." Both men stared ahead, making a point of not looking at one another. When the elevator finally stopped on floor sixteen, the doors opened. Orlando looked at Lefty. "See you around."

Lefty nodded. "Have a nice day."

Orlando exited the elevator first, turning to the right. Lefty knew he had to turn and go left, but worried that Orlando might have figured out the score and would shoot him in the back. Lefty turned left anyway, walking a few steps, and then slowing, turning back to observe his mark. As Orlando was nearing the end of the hall, Lefty turned towards a random door and hovered there, pretending to unlock it. Orlando never looked back, even as he turned and opened a door. He walked through it, disappearing. Lefty turned back towards the door Orlando had gone through. When he reached it, he stood staring at the door for a moment. He pulled out the Glock and raised it, preparing to shoot the lock.

Zip! Zip!

Splinters flew as silenced bullets slammed through the door, missing Lefty's head by mere inches. Lefty moved away from the door, shooting two rounds into the lock. He grabbed the door handle, smashing his way into the room. He expected to dodge more shots, but none came. He looked up, his gun still raised, and saw Orlando crouched behind the bed, his silenced pistol trained on him. Orlando fired again, and Lefty felt a searing pain in his right shoulder. He dove forward, hiding behind this side of the bed, his pistol raised. He couldn't see Orlando and wondered what he was up to.

"I know who you are," Orlando said.

This was news to Lefty. "Oh yeah?"

"You're Spook Collins' boy."

Lefty was momentarily surprised. Before he could sort it out, something shot past the end of the bed in a blur. Lefty instinctively fired a round into it. When the bullet struck the pillow Orlando had thrown, the pillow changed course, flying back in the air like a shot can. Seemingly hundreds of floating white feathers now filled Lefty's vision. That's when Orlando bolted past him, concealed by the feathers, making his way back to the entrance. Lefty peered around the corner, but Orlando was nowhere to be seen. The door was nearly shut, resting there, open just the slightest crack. Lefty knew Orlando was standing in the hall, waiting for him to exit so he could fill him with bullets.

Lefty rocked his body, rolling onto his feet, his Glock raised. He moved around the corner, the gun trained on the door.

"Come on out!" shouted Orlando.

"Fuck you," responded Lefty.

"I won't shoot."

Lefty chuckled to himself. He stood there for the briefest of moments, contemplating his next move. *Here goes nothing*, he thought. He reached out with his left hand, wrapping his fingers around the door handle. The Glock was vertical, ready to come down firing. Lefty pulled the door back about a third of the way, peering out. As he'd expected, Orlando wasn't visible from his vantage point. *Fuck it*, Lefty thought. He leaped out into the hall, his Glock outstretched to his left. When Lefty landed, Orlando was gone.

"Damn," Lefty muttered. He took off running towards the elevators. He couldn't see Orlando, who had obviously boarded one of them. When Lefty reached the two sets of doors, both closed, he saw that the elevator on the left—the one they'd come up in—was on the fifteenth floor, making its way down to the lobby. As Lefty hit the button to summon the other elevator, he saw that one was also on fifteen. Lefty slid his Glock into the shoulder holster. A moment later the doors opened. There was an old white woman wearing square black sunglasses inside. She was holding a small black dog, some sort of terrier that looked like a rat.

Lefty stepped into the elevator.

"You going down to the lobby?" the woman asked.

"Yes, ma'am."

The doors shut, and the elevator came to life. Lefty hoped no one stopped them now. He was pretty sure he'd already lost Orlando, but if the elevator got stopped between here and the lobby, it would be a done deal.

"You're colored," the woman said. "You must be from Detroit."

This took Lefty back for a moment. Even after experiencing a lifetime of racism, he was still stunned by these occurrences, especially when it was done so nonchalantly. He decided to give the old hag a break since she obviously had no idea she was being offensive. "No, ma'am," he said. "I'm from Chicago."

"We're from Miami," the old woman said. "Me and Marvin here." She looked down at the tiny dog staring at Lefty. "Say hi to the colored man." By this time the dog was baring its tiny teeth at him, and soon a growl came rolling up from its throat. The woman looked up at Lefty. "He doesn't normally act that way, but he's not used to coloreds. In our neighborhood, there aren't any. None of our friends even have colored help. They hire the wetbacks for that stuff. But mostly wetbacks are just good for gardening."

Lefty watched the lights above the door that indicated which floor they were on. So far he'd been lucky; the elevator hadn't stopped. They were now passing the tenth floor. He just might see Orlando Williams again.

The old woman said, "My sister Ruthie is on the eighth floor. Maybe I should stop and get her before I take Marvin out to potty." She reached for the button.

"Stop!" blurted Lefty.

The woman was stunned, a deer frozen in headlights. She looked at him, her hand hovering near the button. "What do you mean?"

"Don't hit that button."

Her brow furrowed. "You're gonna rape me, aren't you? I've heard things about these elevators being steel rape traps."

She started to go for the button again.

Lefty pulled out his pistol. "If you push that button, I swear to Jesus I'll blow your goddamn blue-haired head clean the fuck off."

The old woman stared at the gun, shaking her head in disgust. She pulled her hand back.

Marvin growled at Lefty as if he understood what was happening.

"One more thing."

"What?" asked the woman.

"Shut that damned dog up."

"Or what? You'll shoot him?"

Lefty could feel the sweat on his forehead, a result of the hot temperature in the elevator, his fear they would be stopped before reaching the lobby, and his having just sprinted and traded volleys with Orlando.

123

"I swear to God I'll shoot Marvin in the face."

The old woman made a *"hrrrumph"* sound like something from a cartoon. Marvin growled again, trying his best to act vicious. Lefty aimed the Glock at the dog's tiny tennis ball head. "I'm serious," he said. "Shut him up now."

The old woman frowned, but reached down and smacked the dog across its nose. "Be quiet, Marvin," she said. "Be a good boy and I'll give you a treat."

Lefty looked up. The elevator was now approaching the fourth floor.

Marvin was no longer growling. Maybe it was the promise of a treat, but more likely it was the hard smack across its nose. It had always been Lefty's experience that everyone was prone to do the right thing when they got the shit smacked out of them.

"I knew Detroit was a dirty, violent place, but this is shit," said the old woman. "Your people aren't very welcoming. This whole city, this whole filthy place is just a giant shithole."

Lefty said nothing, letting the woman have her say. The elevator was now approaching the second floor. As they passed it, the woman said, "You know what You're no different from any other nigger I've ever met. Every one of you deserve to have your neck in a noose."

Lefty looked down at her with pity. "Why'd you make me do this?" he asked. The woman's face started to twist into a look of confusion about half a second before Lefty's Glock came smashing down across the bridge of her nose. She fell to the floor unconscious, dropping Marvin as she did.

The elevator doors opened at that moment and Marvin bolted through them, scurrying off into the lobby, probably looking to piss somewhere. Lefty walked out. No one was around to see the unconscious old woman. Lefty stared towards the glass doors, seeing Orlando outside now, walking away in the opposite direction from where they'd come. Lefty followed.

When he got outside, Lefty turned to his right just in time to see Orlando turning around the corner of the building. Where the fuck was he going? Lefty broke into a sprint again. *Damn*, he thought. This was too much running for one day, and he was starting to feel the effects. Maybe he needed to lay off the sugar and carbs. When Lefty came to the corner, he pulled out the Glock and turned into the alley. He looked ahead, but couldn't see Orlando. He walked cautiously, gun out in front, wondering where Orlando had gone.

Lefty made it about a third of the way down the alley when a shot zipped past him from a backyard on his left. The bullet struck the hotel next to him, careening off down the alley. Lefty turned towards the yard, instinctively ducking down. He swiveled the pistol towards the yard. He saw nothing but an old boat, an aluminum shed, a yard swing—just the normal backyard crap. He moved cautiously towards the yard, wondering if Orlando had slipped between the houses. As he stepped onto the grass, Orlando emerged from behind the shed, firing. The bullet just missed Lefty. Lefty turned the gun towards Orlando, firing off two quick shots. They banged against the aluminum shed, and Orlando ducked behind it.

Lefty didn't hesitate. He just kept walking ahead like the goddamn Terminator. The Glock was aimed at the corner of the shed. As Lefty approached it, Orlando popped back into sight, now a ways back, and fired another shot. Lefty ducked again, as if that would somehow help. This movement made him momentarily disoriented and Orlando took advantage of the fact, sprinting past the gold fiberglass fishing boat towards the house. Lefty raised the Glock and squeezed off two shots in quick succession. The shots were wide, missing Orlando but striking the boat's hull. Orlando swerved, placing the boat between himself and Lefty, and made his way into the area between the houses. Once again he disappeared from sight.

This motherfucker, thought Lefty. He jogged towards the place where Orlando had been. He moved around the boat just in time to see Orlando turning to the right around the front of the next house. Lefty continued to chase Orlando, now making his way around the house. When he came around the corner, his eyes scanned the area ahead, but he didn't see Orlando. *Shit*. Lefty slowed a bit, his gun out ahead, surveying the area for the bastard. He made his way across a driveway. As he did, Orlando's head and gun popped up from behind the house's concrete steps. Orlando fired another round at Lefty, and Lefty could actually hear the bullet zip past his ear. Lefty kept moving towards Orlando, his gun aimed at him. He squeezed the trigger just as Orlando jumped out from behind the steps, taking off running again. Lefty started to fire, but remembered he needed to conserve his bullets. Orlando ran around a bush at the corner of the house, and disappeared from sight.

Lefty remembered that song about nobody saying there'd be days like these, and found that he agreed with its sentiment. Lefty slowed again as he approached the bush, making his way around the outside instead of the inside where Orlando had disappeared. Lefty came around the bush, but Orlando wasn't there. *What the hell?* Lefty continued around the bush, making sure Orlando wasn't hiding behind it. He wasn't. Just as Lefty started to look up, Orlando squeezed off another shot from between the houses. Lefty moved to his right, hesitating just long enough to consider ducking behind the bush. Instead he kept moving ahead. Orlando was doing this little sideways jog, just sideways enough so he could see what Lefty was doing. He raised his pistol, and Lefty instinctively ducked again. But Orlando didn't fire. He kept running, now in the backyard, and ducked behind a large tree. Lefty powered forward towards him. Orlando emerged, firing a shot, but missed. Lefty broke into a sprint, and Orlando took off away from the tree. He ran along a wooden privacy fence back by the alley. Lefty raised his pistol again, slowing, but realized his heavy panting was causing him to shake enough he wouldn't make the shot. Orlando was running back into the alley, his back now exposed.

Orlando turned to his left, heading towards the parking lot where the Escalade was parked. He disappeared behind the fence. Lefty was panting hard now, but somehow kept moving. He wanted desperately to stop and catch his breath, but there wasn't time.

Damn, he thought. *This motherfucker's got great cardio.*

Lefty powered on, trying to hold his gun out ahead, but it swayed like a branch in a strong wind, occasionally dropping and aiming itself towards the ground. He finally reached the alley, rounding the corner of the fence. He raised the Glock at Orlando just in time to see him turning around the corner of the hotel and back into the parking lot. Lefty gave chase as best he could, winded as he was. After coming around the corner, he saw Orlando approaching the Escalade, doing a half-run, fumbling for his keys with his gun in hand. Lefty slowed, wearing out. As he did, Orlando did too. He stood there in front of the Escalade, fishing out his keys. Just as he came up with them, Lefty fired another shot, this one striking Orlando in the side. Orlando staggered back towards the vehicle, red blood immediately appearing, a stark contrast to his white jacket. Despite having just been shot, Orlando staggered around the vehicle, opening the door and climbing inside. Lefty stood watching him.

As Orlando went to back out, another car pulled into the drive behind him. This left Orlando nowhere to go except back towards Lefty. Lefty could see what he was doing, so he walked over, standing in the middle of the area where Orlando would be driving. Orlando nosed the Escalade around in his direction, now lurching slowly towards Lefty. Lefty raised the Glock towards Orlando's head, and both men locked eyes. Before Lefty could squeeze the trigger, Orlando stomped on the gas and the Escalade came shooting towards Lefty. Lefty fired a shot, hitting the windshield, but missing Orlando. When the shot struck the windshield, the Escalade swerved to the right, scraping against a car. Orlando spun the steering wheel and the Escalade shot towards Lefty. Just as the vehicle was about to make contact, Lefty threw himself onto its hood. He was now looking down through the glass at his adversary.

Orlando swerved to his right, and then his left, scraping the Escalade along a number of vehicles in the hopes of shaking Lefty from the hood. But Lefty hung on for dear life. The Glock in his hand made it difficult to hold on, but somehow he managed. Once they were out of the parking lot and into the side street, Orlando stomped the brake, trying to lose his unwanted passenger. But Lefty held on, peering in at Orlando. Neither man was flustered the way most people would be in this situation. Orlando, calm and cool, drove the Escalade up over the curb, but Lefty hung on. Although Lefty couldn't see what was happening behind him, the Escalade ran a stop sign and shot out into the busy street in front of the hotel. Orlando swerved, narrowly avoiding a pickup truck coming from the left.

Lefty now focused on the pistol in his hand. He looked at it, as if watching the movement of his hand would somehow help. At that moment, before Lefty could manage anything, Orlando turned on the windshield wipers, which slid into action, hitting Lefty's hand holding the gun. The other wiper came rumbling up from beneath Lefty's torso, scraping across his stomach. After having struck Lefty's body, both wipers were stuck there, continuously pushing against his body.

Lefty moved his right hand slightly, concentrating on bringing the gun around to fire through the windshield. He saw Orlando's eyes, watching his movements. Lefty slid the gun up the glass a bit, moving it over the spot where Orlando's head was. Lefty looked at Orlando, thinking he had him now, when he saw the hitman smile.

The fuck?

That was when the Escalade slammed into the back of a UPS truck that was stopped in the street, preparing to turn. The impact threw Lefty backwards against the top of the truck. Lefty crashed hard against its edge, injuring his ribs, and maybe breaking them. He fell to the street, dropping his Glock, just as Orlando backed up the Escalade. Lefty landed on his ass. He thought of grabbing the gun, even though is body hurt like hell. He looked up at the front of the Escalade, realizing that in the moment it would take to grab the pistol and try to level it towards Orlando, Orlando would smash him between the two vehicles.

The Escalade was stopped for the briefest of moments. At the exact moment Orlando stomped on the gas, Lefty rolled to his right. The Escalade shot forward, turning to its right, away from Lefty. Orlando scraped the nose of the vehicle against the right corner of the truck. Lefty fell over in the street, reaching out for the pistol lying on the pavement, but came up short. As he did, he saw the Escalade disappear around the truck.

Lefty wiggled his body forward, retrieving the Glock. At that moment, a young black UPS driver staggered around the truck. He stood over Lefty as Lefty scraped himself up off the pavement, slowly climbing to his feet. The UPS driver put his hand out to assist Lefty. Lefty put out his right hand, pistol still in it. The UPS driver wrapped his hand around both Lefty's hand and the gun, pulling him to his feet. "You alright?" managed the driver.

For a moment both men wobbled there, as if they were trying to stand still in the midst of an earthquake. Now getting his bearings, Lefty looked past the stunned UPS driver', seeing a silver Prius edging around them slowly. The man driving the vehicle had his window down. He pulled up beside them. "Are you guys okay? I saw what happened—"

Before he could finish, Lefty raised the Glock, aiming it point blank at his face. "Get out," he said, surprised at the calmness of his voice. The generic-looking middle-aged driver looked flustered, but kind of shrugged, realizing there was nothing else he could do. He climbed out of the Prius. As he did, Lefty kept the gun in his face. He extended his arm, pointing the gun past the man. "Move over there." The man did as he was told. As he did, Lefty turned and backed towards the open car door. He swiveled the gun towards the UPS driver. Lefty turned and jumped into the Prius, cramming himself into its tight space. He shifted it into drive and the tiny vehicle came to life, speeding away.

NINE
HE IS RISEN!

When Lefty got back to his Caddy, he could see two police cars parked in front of the hotel. One of them had the flashing blue lights, the other did not. There were a couple of looky-loos congregated, and he could see a single uniformed cop; the others were presumably inside, talking with hotel management. Lefty parked the Prius on the right side of the street, opposite the Caddy. The curb was painted yellow to indicate there was no parking, but that was the least of Lefty's concerns. He opened the door and got out, leaving the keys in the ignition.

Lefty looked past the Caddy at the gathering in front of the Dumont, making sure no one saw him. They didn't. Lefty casually unlocked the driver's side door of the Caddy and climbed in. Now behind the wheel, he started the ignition and the O'Jays once again came to life.

Lefty looked in the rear-view mirror, seeing the scratches on his face. This had been a hell of a day. He dropped the Caddy into drive and moved towards the busy street, turning right and passing the hotel. As he did, he looked at the crowd and the cops, but no one looked at him.

As he drove, he thought about Orlando. He'd shot him in the side, but he doubted that would slow him down much. After all, the man was a legend. He wondered if he would see him again. Maybe, just maybe, he and Brooks would be able to finish the job before Orlando could get a chance to make his move. But Lefty doubted it. He was pretty sure he would see the man again, and he knew there would be trouble when he did.

He looked at the sack of cold coneys sitting in the passenger's seat. Lefty considered them. He'd developed an appetite chasing Orlando around the Dumont, so he decided to have another. It wouldn't do much to help his cardio, but at this point Lefty didn't care. He reached over with his right arm—the one with the bullet in its shoulder—and slid a coney from the sack. He tlid the wrapper off the dog and ate it. *Not bad*, he thought, chowing down. Even after having sat in the sun for an hour, the coney was still pretty damned good.

As he drove, the O'Jays now singing "Let Me Make Love to You," Lefty kept a close eye on the rear-view mirror, fully expecting the cops to show up at any minute. He wondered if the Dumont had caught the shootout on camera. In this day and age, pretty much every business had a camera, so he assumed the answer was yes.

Lefty was a couple blocks away from the motel where Brooks and Dixie were keeping Layla. He stopped at a light. He had been driving with both windows down, and he could now hear screaming outside. He looked over at the sidewalk beside him and saw a dirty old gray-haired black man standing there holding a sign. It read: "HE IS RISEN!" The old man saw him looking. He stopped yelling for a moment and stepped off the curb, leaning towards the Caddy's passenger-side window. "Hey, young brother," he said, grinning big, every other tooth missing. "Can you loan me ten dollars?"

Lefty smiled. "I don't have ten dollars."

The old man's expression instantly changed to one of anger. *"You mean to tell me you're driving a goddamn Cadillac and you don't have ten dollars? Bullshit!"*

Lefty flipped the switch, rolling the window up. The old man screamed, *"Fuck you, man! Fuck you in your goddamn face!"* He was flipping Lefty off, putting his finger against the window.

The light changed and Lefty drove away, leaving the old man standing there to wait for the rapture alone.

WHEN LEFTY PULLED into the parking lot of the motel, he didn't have a care in the world. He just wanted to go in and take a shower and relax. But when he looked at the outside of Brooks' room, he knew that wasn't an option.

There were two men, both tough-looking SOBs, leading Brooks, Dixie, and Layla into an old beat up black van of the "I've got candy" pedo variety. But these weren't pedophiles; these were second-rate goombas, obviously Bruno De Lorenzo's goons. Lefty couldn't see their guns, but he knew they were there. There was no way Brooks or Dixie would allow themselves to be herded into that van without a fear of being killed. Lefty was certain there would be a third man man inside the van, to sit behind the captives and keep them under control.

He looked at Layla climbing into the van. She looked scared, and that frightened Lefty. But not just fear; he was angry now. *Really fucking pissed.* No one fucked with his Layla and lived to see another day. That was one of Lefty's hard-fast rules, like not eating after eight p.m. and never

ANDY RAUSCH

watching a movie starring Adam Sandler. Lefty didn't wanna be seen, so he pulled around through the parking lot, past the black van, trying to look nonchalant like he didn't notice . He drove through the lot, parking down near the front office. He was just far enough away he could park without drawing suspicion, but still close enough he could watch the van. Of course he was now on the other side of it, so he could no longer see the captives being forced inside.

A few minutes later, one of the goombas came around the van and into view, climbing into the driver's side. The van backed out of its parking spot, turning in Lefty's direction. They didn't pay him any mind sitting there, and they passed by him, exiting onto the busy street. Lefty pulled out and followed them. This was the most car chasing Lefty had ever done. He felt like a regular Steve McQueen.

He let the black van get way up ahead so its driver would have no idea they were being followed. Realizing it was time for a change, Lefty popped out the O'Jays CD and replaced it with Curtis Mayfield. A moment later, "Little Child Runnin' Wild" came on, and the world was right again. At least as right as it could seem with his Layla up there in that pedo van with a gun in her face. But Lefty was determined to do something about that. Come hell or high water, he would save his Tator Tot. He watched as the van turned, down a busy cross street. Lefty also turned, following at a safe distance. A few minutes passed, and the van hooked a left on a nondescript side street. Lefty followed.

The neighborhood was upscale, the street lined with middling-sized, mostly white Colonial-style houses. They were big by Lefty's standards, but he knew these were far from the biggest houses in town. No, this was the rich but not filthy-rich neighborhood. Lefty glanced at some of the houses, wondering if any black people lived on this street. He doubted it. It didn't look inviting, somehow screaming "NO NIGGERS" while simultaneously being bland and low-key.

Lefty was a ways behind the van, which seemed out of place here, when it pulled into a driveway in front of one of the big white houses. The driver's door popped open, and the goon hopped out, heading around the vehicle. Lefty drove slowly, just faster than idle, but was forced to pass the driveway so he wouldn't draw attention. As he passed, he could see Goon #2 on the other side of the van opening the side door to let the captives out. Lefty drove about four houses down, pulling over on the right side of the road. He took a deep breath and turned off the ignition. He climbed out, walked around to the trunk, and popped it open. He stood over it, ejecting the half-spent clip from the Glock and letting it fall to the pavement. He reached in and retrieved a clip, putting it in the right pocket of his jacket. He grabbed a second clip, and slid it into the pistol. He closed the trunk, turning back towards the house. As he did, he saw Brooks, Dixie, and Layla being taken inside by two of the goons. The third goon was now in the van, backing out of the driveway. It turned in the opposite direction from where Lefty was, driving into the distance.

Lefty started walking towards the house, his Glock by his side. He must have been quite a sight, walking down the street of this white bread neighborhood, a bleeding black man carrying a Glock. Lefty wondered if his murderous, vengeful intent would be visible to someone seeing him objectively. Was that a thing a person could identify? Lefty believed it was, proud that if that was, he now personified that.

As he approached the house, he scanned the area, trying

to decide his next move. There was no one outside. He had seen two goons enter, but he felt relatively sure there were more inside. What was this place? Obviously it was a house, but what was its purpose? Or did it have a purpose? Was this a sort of safe house where they held (and probably tortured) captives, or was this just one of their own personal houses? Lefty thought it an odd location for a torture house, it being smack dab in the middle of the city in a nice neighborhood. Lefty had never possessed a torture house, but he was pretty sure if he did it would be out in the country somewhere where no one could see or hear anything.

Lefty came to the driveway, making his way up towards the house.

Fuck it, he thought. *Let's do this.*

He would walk right up to the front door and knock like he was the Jehovah's Witnesses here to offer them a copy of *The Watchtower*. Lefty was now on the porch in front of the door. There was no need to knock as there was a doorbell. He pushed it, hearing its loud chimes inside. A moment later the door opened and a thirty-something Italian guy was there, peering out through a crack.

"Who you supposed to be?"

"candy-gram," said Lefty.

This perplexed the guy. Before he could voice his confusion, Lefty kicked the door, sending the guy flying back. Before the man hit the floor, Lefty fired a shot center mass through his chest. He stepped into the house, over the dead man, looking ahead. There was a couch along the far wall. Dixie and Brooks were sitting there, next to a goomba smoking a cigarette. The man's cigarette started to fall from his lips, but just dangled there now. He moved forward to stand, but Lefty raised his arm and fired a second shot through his forehead.

Brooks started to climb to his feet. Lefty looked at him. "Where's Layla?"

Brooks moved his head, motioning towards an open doorway leading to the dining room. Lefty made his way into the room, scanning it thoroughly, seeing no one. He looked to the right and saw a hallway. Almost the second he looked, another goon emerged with Layla, his pistol aimed at her temple. She looked terrified. She wasn't crying yet, but was on the verge. The man was pushing her, moving her down the hall towards Lefty.

Lefty made eye contact with her. "You okay, Tator Tot?"

"Yeah," said Layla, sniffling. "But this guy's an asshole." She paused. "Can I say that word, Daddy?"

"Sure," said Lefty. "It seems appropriate."

Layla said, "He thinks 'Rocket Man' is about Elton John being gay."

Lefty, standing there with his pistol trained on the man's face, laughed despite himself.

"What's so funny?" asked the man. "It totally is."

"Is not," argued Layla.

"Is too," said the man defensively. "He says he's not the guy that people think he is. He says that he's a rocket man." He looked up at Lefty. "You get it, right? A *rocket* man. When he says 'rocket' he's referring to dick. He's saying he likes dick and that he's gay." He paused for a moment before asking, "What do you think?"

Lefty squeezed the trigger, answering the question, ensuring that "Rocket Man," dicks, and the bullet would be the last things going through the guy's head.

The man fell to the floor and Layla came running towards Lefty. *"Daddy!"* she squealed. She ran to him, wrapping her arms around him, but Lefty was looking for the next man to kill.

Layla leaned back, looking at his shoulder. "What happened to your arm, Daddy? You're bleeding."

"Daddy got a boo-boo," he said, seeing someone through the sliding-glass doors. He stared out, seeing one of the goons running past.

"You didn't get a boo-boo," said Layla. "You got shot."

Lefty didn't have time for this right now. He turned towards the backdoor. He'd be damned if he was gonna let the guy get away after they'd taken Layla captive. No one got away with that shit. Not ever.

Lefty moved Layla out of his way. "I'll be right back, Tator Tot. Daddy's gotta do something."

He moved to the door and slid it open, moving through it quickly. The guy was still running, going around the house. Lefty broke into his twelve-billionth sprint of the day. *Fucking cardio*, he thought. When Lefty came to the corner of the house, rounding it, the guy took a shot at him. The bullet struck the house, burying itself in its side. Lefty raised his silenced pistol and fired at the man, who broke into a run again. Lefty gave chase, taking the corner quickly. He dodged another bullet just before the dumbass disappeared back into the house through the front door.

Really? This is the fucking game we're playing?

Lefty stopped for a second, catching his breath. Then he remembered that Layla was still in the house. He made his way quickly past the front of the house and onto the porch, going through the front door. When he did, he saw another of an apparently endless supply of goons standing over the couch with a gun on Brooks and Dixie, who were sitting captive again. Before Lefty could react, he heard "drop it" from his left. He turned, now seeing another goomba fuck standing there with a .38.

Lefty dropped the Glock onto a maroon throw rug. He looked at the guy, who was smiling big. The guy said, "Come on in. You think you're pretty big shit, huh?"

Lefty feigned a grin. "Yeah, pretty big shit. That's me."

"Well," the man said. "You're about to be dead shit."

Lefty looked at him, his expression changing to one of disappointment. *"Really, dude?"*

The man didn't understand. "What?"

"You sure that's the line you wanna go with, 'dead shit'?"

Lefty heard Brooks chuckling.

The man asked, "What do you mean?"

"That's lame as fuck."

The guy started to say something in his defense when Brooks spoke up. "He's right. That's the worst goddamn line I ever heard in my life. I've been killing people for a lot of decades now and I can't remember anyone ever trying on a line as stupid as that."

The goomba standing by the couch barked, *"Shut your mouth, old man!"*

Brooks shrugged, saying nothing.

The guy holding the gun on Lefty said, "Seriously, I'm about to kill you deader than fuck." He repositioned his pistol. "You're about to go down for the count, nigger."

Lefty braced himself, seeing the man's finger tighten on the trigger.

Bam! Bam! came the shots.

Two things occurred to Lefty in that millisecond: he didn't feel any pain, and the guy's expression contorted into something strange and unidentifiable. And then the guy fell to the ground, the .38 falling to the floor beside the Glock.

Lefty looked up and saw Layla standing in the doorway to the next room, holding a smoking pistol.

"Oh, hon," said Dixie.

The goomba standing over her and Brooks turned towards Layla, about to take a shot at her. Before he could aim the pistol, Lefty rushed him, slamming him to the ground. As they collided with the floor, the gun went off, firing into the wall behind Dixie's head. Lefty grabbed the man's pistol hand, wrestling him for control. They writhed around on the floor. Lefty was stronger, and he could feel himself slowly making progress. The man was staring at the gun. Seeing he was distracted, Lefty slammed his forehead into the man's face, breaking his nose. The man let out a guttural sound and blood began pouring from his nostrils. The goomba was confused and disoriented. Despite his forehead hurting like hell, Lefty slammed it into the guy's face again, smashing the back of his head into the wooden floor.

"You want me to shoot him, Daddy?" asked Layla, standing over them, still holding the gun.

"No, Tator Tot," said Lefty. "Daddy's got this."

As the two men continued to wrestle, Brooks stood up. Lefty couldn't see what the old man was doing as he was busy wrestling. A moment later, Brooks' feet were beside their heads.

"Lean back," said Brooks.

Lefty didn't understand.

The man on the ground looked up at Brooks, confused.

Brooks became angry. *"I said lean back, goddammit!"*

Lefty leaned back away from the goon. As he did, Brooks raised his foot and stomped down hard against the man's face, burying his heel in it. Lefty had a front-row seat to the man's destruction. To hammer home the point,

Brooks raised his foot and stomped on the man's face again, completely crushing his skull.

"Well, hell, Brooks," said Lefty, now sitting up.

"What?"

"You sure killed the hell out of that guy."

"I guess so."

"Typical Brooks," said Dixie, audibly irritated. "You always gotta go too far."

Brooks looked at her, an annoyed expression on his face. "What are you going on about, woman?"

"You didn't need to do all that."

"What?" asked Brooks. "The guy had it coming."

"He did, but you went overboard like you always do. You brought a bazooka to a knife fight."

Brooks shrugged. "I won't apologize for what I did. It got the job done."

"Of course you won't apologize," said Dixie. "You *never* apologize."

"Bullshit," said Brooks. "I used to apologize all the time. It feels like the only thing I ever did when we were together."

Dixie looked at Lefty. "You wanna hear a typical Brooks Barker apology? He would say the wrong thing and piss me off. Then he would say something like, 'I'm sorry you're mad.' He wouldn't take responsibility for any of it. He was never sorry for the thing he did, he was just sorry that I was mad. He put all the blame on me."

"Fiddlesticks," Brooks said.

"*Fiddlesticks?*" asked Lefty. "How the hell old are you?"

Brooks looked at him. "What's that supposed to mean?"

"No one under the age of 264 should ever use the word 'fiddlesticks.'"

Dixie laughed. Layla was standing there, still holding the pistol. "What is fiddlesticks, Daddy?"

"It's just a made-up word that old men use," said Dixie.

Brooks rolled his eyes.

"Does that mean Brooks is old?" asked Layla.

"The man was there when they invented dirt," said Lefty.

Layla didn't understand. "What does that mean?"

"It means he's really fucking old, kid," said Dixie.

AFTER STOPPING at the pharmacy to get medical supplies, they returned to the motel, where Dixie skillfully removed the bullet from Lefty's shoulder. They had considered going somewhere else and getting new rooms since De Lorenzo's goons knew where to find them, but they decided against it. "I'd like to see them try that shit again," said Lefty. "I'll send every single one of 'em to hell."

"I thought you didn't believe in hell," said Brooks.

"It's hyperbole," said Lefty. "There really is nowhere else for me to say I'd send 'em that sounds quite so menacing."

"Except Detroit, and we're already there." Brooks looked over at Layla, who was sitting criss-cross-apple-sauce on the bed, coloring.

"Dixie, why did you hate Spook?" asked Lefty.

Dixie looked at him incredulously. "Is that some kind of joke?"

"No, I was just wondering."

"Have you met the man?"

"Oh, I've met him," said Lefty. "And I hate him too, but I know the reasons I hate him. I just wondered why you hated him."

Dixie pondered this for a moment before saying, "He was the meanest sonofabitch I ever met, and I was married to a real prick." Lefty and Dixie both looked at Brooks and chuckled. Brooks just shrugged. "Spook was argumentative and he hated women," continued Dixie. "He was a real piece of work, that man."

"Do you think I'm like him?" asked Lefty.

"Fuck no," said Dixie. "Do you *wanna* be like him?"

"Fuck no."

Brooks spoke up, changing the subject. "Now that we know the Professor is here, we'd better get Bruno De Lorenzo taken care of as quickly as possible. Do you think he'll go after him tonight?"

"No," said Lefty. "He's shot up, too, and he's gonna be exhausted from all the running around and shooting we did. We did a lot of running."

"When do you wanna do this thing?" asked Brooks.

"Bright and early in the morning," said Lefty. "They won't expect it."

It was just after eleven when the phone rang, waking Lefty. He reached out and grabbed it from its cradle. He put it to his ear, still half asleep. "Hello?" he managed.

A voice on the other end said, "Is this the nigger?"

Now Lefty was fully awake. He sat up, holding the phone to his ear. He looked over at Layla, lying there asleep.

"Who the fuck is this?"

"Maybe you've heard of me," said the voice. "My name is Bruno De Lorenzo."

TEN

UP JUMPS THE DEVIL

B RUNO D E L ORENZO was in Mikey Cantore's basement, lording over him. Mikey was the son of a feared mob captain, but Bruno wasn't afraid. He didn't give a shit if Mikey was the son of Zeus. Mikey could have been the son of Genghis Fucking Khan and it wouldn't have saved him from the things Bruno was about do. Bruno looked down at Mikey, sitting there tied to a wooden chair with tears streaming down his face.

"Remember when I told you there would be a time and place to talk about what happened today?" asked Bruno.

Mikey nodded.

"Now is that time."

Mikey stared silently, unsure what to say or do. Bruno waited a moment before becoming enraged and kicking him in the chest. Mikey's chair tipped back and over. He was now lying there on the floor, crying and looking helpless and pathetic, like a whale stuck on the shore.

Bruno stood over him, looking down at the sorry fuck.

"I said talk, goddammit!" he screamed.

Mikey looked up, fear visible in his eyes.

"I was at the house with the old people and the little girl," said Mikey.

"Go on..."

"Well," Mikey said weakly, "the black guy showed up—"

"The nigger," corrected Bruno.

"Right, the nigger. He showed up."

"Then what happened?"

"He...he..."

"Yes?" asked Bruno.

"He started shooting everybody."

Bruno's eyes narrowed, a sadistic look on his face. "Except you."

Mikey said nothing.

"Why do you think that is?" asked Bruno. "How did you happen to survive when no one else did?"

"I went out the backdoor before he saw me."

Bruno walked around the toppled chair, pushing his foot down hard against Mikey's chest. "You ran away like a little bitch," said Bruno. "Isn't that the truth? You made like Jesse Owens and ran the fuck outta there."

"I escaped," said Mikey.

Bruno applied more pressure. "Say it."

Mikey cried out as Bruno pressed his foot into his chest. When Bruno eased up, Mikey relented and said, "I ran away."

"Like a little bitch," said Bruno.

"Like a little bitch," repeated Mikey.

"So they all got away, the old people and the niggers."

"I don't know. I assume so."

"You don't know because you ran away like a fucking coward."

Bruno looked across the room at Dom and Pino, who

were leaning silently against the brick wall. "Come over here and get this fucker back upright."

The two goons moved forward, flanking Mikey. They leaned down, each of them grabbing an arm, and pulled him up. As they did, Bruno stepped back to make room, accidentally stepping on the foot of Mikey's cocker spaniel. Bruno looked down at the dog. "You got a dog, huh? What's the little fuckstick's name?"

Mikey blinked. "My dog?"

"No, Ike Turner's dog, you fuckin' moron," said Bruno. "What do you think I mean?"

"Her name is Hillary."

Bruno stared at him dumbfounded. "Like Hillary Clinton?"

"Right," said Mikey. "I named him after her."

"I fucking hate that bitch."

Mikey's expression changed. "Please don't hurt my dog."

"You think I'd do that?" asked Bruno. He stared into Mikey's eyes. He reached back and slapped him hard across the face. "I'm not mad at your dog, even if she has the stupid fucking name of a cunt. You made the mistake, Mikey, you pay the price. Not her. It's not her fault she's got a dumb motherfucker for an owner."

"Thank you for not hurting her," said Mikey.

"Don't thank me yet," said Bruno. "You and me, we got more business between us." He looked at Pino. "Did you bring in the stuff from the car?"

Pino said nothing. Instead he started rifling through his pockets. He pulled his hand out, producing a large pocket knife. He handed it to Dom. Pino then went back to searching through his pockets, this time producing a pair of silver pliers. He handed them to Bruno.

Bruno smiled big. "This makes me happy, like the Fourth of Goddamn July, you know that, Mikey?"

Mikey's eyes were big now and he was trembling. "No, Bruno," he said. "Please don't kill me. Please. Please don't. I'll—"

"Hold still," interrupted Bruno. He nodded to Pino, who grabbed Mikey's head, locking it like he was putting him in a sleeper hold. Bruno leaned in towards Mikey's face. Mikey could smell garlic on his breath.

"Open your mouth," said Bruno.

Mikey clamped his lips shut, refusing to open them.

Bruno became angry. "You want me to kill your dog, real slow-like? Cause I'll do it. Open your goddamn mouth now or Hillary dies a long, excruciating, painful-as-fuck death like nothing you can imagine. Trust me, it'll be one for the ages."

Mikey nervously opened his mouth. Bruno didn't skip a beat. He immediately shoved the open pliers into Mikey's mouth, locking them around his tongue. Mikey made a loud, terrified noise, but it was to no avail. Mikey was fucked ten ways to Tuesday and he knew it. Bruno stretched Mikey's tongue out of his mouth as far as it would reach. He looked at Dom, who understood. Dom opened the pocket knife and put its blade against Bruno's tongue. He started to saw through the meaty tongue, but the blade was so sharp that the tongue came loose in Dom's hand in about twenty seconds.

Mikey was thrashing around now, trying to scream, but could only manage a prolonged guttural sound. Still, even without a tongue to scream, the awful moan did the job conveying his pain.

Bruno sat the pliers down on Mikey's lap. As Mikey continued to moan that loud awful moan, Bruno squatted down beside Hillary. He started stroking the dog's head. "There, there," he said assuringly. "That's a good dog." Hillary was enjoying the petting, moving her head around to meet Bruno's hand as it ran over her.

Bruno looked up at Dom. "Hand it over."

Dom reached across in front of Mikey, still moaning, and handed the bloody, saliva-covered tongue to his boss. Bruno took the tongue and held it in front of the cocker spaniel's nose. "Good girl," he said. "That's a good girl. Who wants to eat daddy's tongue?" Hillary sniffed at it for a matter of moments. Finally, after a minute or so, she opened her mouth and leaned in, snapping up Mikey's tongue. She lowered herself back down close to the ground and started chewing the bloody meat. As she did, Bruno laughed. He turned to Mikey, grinning big. "Cat got your tongue, Mikey? Aww, no, it's your fuckin' dog. Would ya look at that? She's eatin' your fuckin' tongue like it's Alpo!"

Mikey was rocking a little in his ropes, moaning a low moan like an angry cat about to battle. Bruno looked at Dom. "Do me a favor," he said. "Cut Mikey here's arms loose." Dom looked at Bruno questioningly. "Nah," said Bruno, "cut him loose." Dom shrugged, and then leaned in, sawing at the ropes. Sharp or no, it took the blade significantly longer to cut through the ropes than it had taken to cut through Mikey's tongue. After a couple of minutes, the ropes were cut.

"Get him on his feet," said Bruno.

Dom and Pino flanked Mikey again, lifting him out of the chair.

Bruno walked to the stairs. "Bring the little faggot this way. We're gonna take him upstairs."

Bruno led the way, with the Dom, Pino, and Mikey following. Mikey was swaying, still moaning, and Dom and

Pino were propping him up. When Bruno was almost to the top of the stairs, he turned back to look at Mikey. "Bet you never thought you'd see upstairs again," he said, grinning sadistically. "You never know, maybe I'll let you go." He laughed at his own joke.

Once they were all upstairs, Bruno led them into the kitchen.

"You got a nice kitchen here," said Bruno. "Real nice place. You got the whole kitchen island, all these nice appliances."

Mikey was going into shock from the pain. He moaned continually.

"Bring him over here," said Bruno, motioning to the sink.

The two goons pushed Mikey towards it. He was facing the sink. They pushed him all the way up against it. "Grab his dick-beater," said Bruno.

Dom grabbed Mikey's hand and held it up.

"You remember that night you had us all over to watch the Superbowl?" asked Bruno. "You remember that? The fucking Patriots won again, but what can you do? They always win, right?"

Mikey stared at him, whimpering.

"Two things happened that night," said Bruno. "You know what they were?"

Mikey said nothing.

"The first thing was I fucked your wife and she gave me head in your bathroom. Did you know that? Think back, Mikey. Did you kiss her that night?"

Mikey said nothing.

"The second wasn't really a thing that happened so much as it was something I noticed," said Bruno. "I noticed that you had this fancy garbage disposal. I remember it because I was thinking I really need to get one. I didn't even know they still made those. We had one when I was a kid, but..."

Mikey knew what was coming. He tried to get free, but the goons were holding him down. Bruno was holding his hand. Mikey made a long moaning sound just before Bruno crammed his hand down into the garbage disposal. Bruno used his other hand to switch it on, and the garbage disposal came whirring to life, making a clunking noise as it cut through Mikey's flesh and bone. After a few seconds of going slow and making that clunking sound, it regained its regular speed. Mikey tried to scream, moaning louder than ever.

Bruno leaned in close, staring into his eyes. "You think we're done, cocksucker? Oh, no, we ain't done until I say so." Bruno looked at Dom. "Did you bring the other thing?"

Dom walked around Mikey, heading for the backdoor. As he did, Pino grabbed him tightly to compensate for Dom's absence. Bruno looked at Pino. "Let's do the other hand now. Fuckin' guy needs a matched set. What good's one hand anyway?"

Bruno grabbed Mikey's surviving hand and went through the same steps, chopping it off in the garbage disposal. Mikey was gyrating now like a crazy person. Pino was holding onto him, but only loosely. Bruno looked into the garbage disposal. "Guess what?" he said. "This garbage disposal is dirty. You really should clean it. It's filled with hands!"

Pino chuckled. Now Dom returned, carrying a green plastic gas can. Bruno held Mikey's arm stumps out over the sink. He looked at Dom, who was unscrewing the lid. "Pour the gas all over his wounds," Bruno said. He looked at

Mikey. "Don't worry, pal, this won't hurt a bit. It's like medicine. It'll make it all better."

Dom poured the gasoline, completely dousing Mikey's wounds. Mikey let out a loud moan as Bruno laughed maniacally.

As Dom and Pino finished the job, the buzzing sound of a chainsaw loud inside the house, Bruno sat in the dark on the back steps, smoking a cigar. When the chainsaw finally quieted, he reached into his pocket and removed his cell phone. He pushed a button, calling the number he'd programmed earlier. The phone rang twice before a man answered. "Hello?"

"Is this the nigger?" asked Bruno.

Lefty was sitting up in his bed in the dark, looking over at the sleeping Layla as he spoke.

"What do you want?"

Bruno chuckled. "You know what I want. I want your ass, and not in a faggy kinda way, but in an icepick through your eyes kinda way."

"Fuck you," spat Lefty.

"Can I ask you a question, nigger?"

Lefty said nothing. After a brief silence, Bruno spoke again. "Have you heard about what I did to Joe Abelli and his bratty cunt of a daughter? I'll bet you have. Everyone knows that story. I'm sort of proud of that one, honestly. It'll be my legacy. I could work hard at this shit for the rest of my life and I'll never top that."

"It doesn't matter," said Lefty. "You won't be living long."

Bruno laughed. "Think about what I did to that little girl, nigger. Now imagine what I can do to your kid. You know what they say, nigger kids get twice."

"Who says that?"

Bruno laughed. "I do."

Lefty stared at the sleeping Layla.

"If you touch her, I'll—"

"Kill me?" asked Bruno. "How droll. What should I do, nigger? You tell me. Should I try something new and try and outdo that whole Abelli thing, or should I dip into my catalog and play a little something from my greatest hits? You know, I almost let my guy Pino have sex with Abelli's kid. Pretty gross, huh? I wouldn't have done that. It was against everything I believe in. But you know what? For you I'll make an exception. I'll let all the guys in my crew have their way with your little girl. What do you think about that? And you know, just for you, I might even have to get in on that myself."

Lefty started to tell Bruno about the various ways he would torture and murder him, but Bruno hung up.

ELEVEN
SHIT HAPPENS

IT WAS AROUND six in the morning when Lefty, Brooks, Dixie, and Layla walked across the street to McDonald's. They discussed the job while they ate. Despite having been awake most of the night, Lefty didn't mention Bruno's call, feeling that mentioning it somehow sullied Layla. As they sat and talked, Lefty said, "Dixie, I would like you to stay at the motel and watch Layla."

He knew at once he'd said the wrong thing. Dixie immediately became pissed. *"What?"* she asked. "And leave all the killing to the big strong men? Why? Because I'm just a poor little weak woman? Because all I'm capable of doing is cooking and cleaning and watching kids?"

Brooks chimed in. "We all know that's bullshit, woman. You couldn't cook or clean to save your life."

Before she could respond, Lefty said, "I'd really like Layla to be somewhere safe."

"Then you stay behind and watch her little ass," said Dixie.

Lefty exhaled, pausing briefly before saying, "This job was my idea. I brought this to you. This is my goddamn job.

I'll be damned if I miss out on it." He paused before adding, "I wanna be the one who kills Bruno De Lorenzo."

Dixie said, "Why can't Brooks stay back at the motel and watch the kid?"

Brooks laughed. Dixie looked at him.

"What's so funny, Brooks?" she asked. "It was okay if I stayed behind, but somehow the thought of you staying behind is ridiculous?"

"None of this is helping," said Lefty, wondering if the level of irritation and annoyance he was feeling came through in his voice.

"Well, here's an idea," Dixie said. "How about you leave your goddamn kid at home next time you go out on a job to kill gangsters? How about that, huh?"

Lefty looked at Layla, who was oblivious, reading an *Incredible Hulk*.

Brooks reached over and put his hand on Dixie's wrist, trying to calm her. But Dixie wasn't having it. She waved him away. "You get your goddamn hand off my wrist unless you wanna lose it, Brooks Barker."

Brooks pulled his hand back as if it was about to touch fire.

"Could you please calm down?" he asked.

Dixie stared at him with daggers in her eyes. "That kind of shit is the reason I left your ass."

"What does that mean?"

"It means I'd like to have a man who could calm me down without telling me to calm down."

Brooks looked at her, amazed by what he was hearing. "What then? How do you express to someone that you want them to calm down without asking them to calm down?"

"Maybe you could just slap 'em across the face like you did that time in Minnesota," she spat.

"That was one goddamn time," said Brooks. "It was a mistake and I admit it. I fucked up. But don't let that one thing overshadow everything else. That wasn't typical of our marriage. We were together for decades, Dixie, and that only happened once."

And so on.

SEEING NO OTHER OPTION, Lefty finally opted to take Layla with him on the De Lorenzo hit. The compromise they'd reached was that Dixie would sit with her in the lobby. Dixie had only agreed to do this after Lefty finally caved in and told her about De Lorenzo's call. This arrangement would be safer for Layla, and Dixie could shoot anyone who tried to escape. "As long as I get to kill *somebody*, I don't care," she said. "That's the whole reason I came. It's not about the money, it's about the killing. I haven't got to kill anybody in a long-ass time."

They were in the Caddy now, and Lefty ejected the Curtis Mayfield CD. He needed mood music, something appropriate for the situation at hand. He slid in Tupac, playing "If I Die Tonight." Brooks made a face, confused by what he was hearing. Then he looked back at Layla, rapping along verbatim, talking about killing various "motherfuckers." Before he could comment, Dixie spoke up. "Your Daddy lets you talk that way?"

Layla looked at her. "Daddy says it's okay to say motherfucker as long as we're listening to Tupac."

Lefty looked back at her in the rear-view mirror. "Or Ice Cube."

"Right," said the little girl, nodding. "Or Ice Cube."

Brooks asked in earnest, "What exactly is a Tupac?"

Layla giggled. "Dixie's right. You really are old."

Everyone in the car laughed except Brooks, who was still wondering what a Tupac was.

"Layla?" said Lefty.

"Yes, Daddy?"

"I love you very much. I want you to sit in the lobby and do whatever Dixie tells you to do."

"Where will you be?"

"Upstairs, Tator Tot."

"Killing people?"

Lefty paused, unsure what to say.

"Only bad people," said Dixie. "Nobody anyone worth a damn will miss."

Layla looked at her dad in the mirror. "So it's okay to kill people if they're bad?"

"Well," Lefty began weakly.

Brooks interrupted. "Some people are so bad you can't do anything else but kill them. They're like a rabid dog, you gotta put them down."

"Am I gonna kill people someday?" asked Layla.

Lefty found himself speechless. Dixie spoke up. "You already did. You killed the hell out of that man yesterday."

"Yeah, but he was gonna shoot my daddy. It's okay to shoot someone if they're gonna hurt the people you love, right?"

Lefty paused again before saying, "That's right, Tator Tot. If someone is gonna hurt your friends or family, you've gotta do whatever it takes to protect them."

"So you shoot them, right Daddy?"

Brooks said, "Sure thing, kid. You blow their cunt asses away."

. . .

Soon they were at the Belmont Hotel, residence of asshole extraordinaire Bruno De Lorenzo, and Lefty couldn't wait to come face-to-face with the guy. Lefty parked the Caddy in the parking lot. There were no goons visible from the parking lot. In fact, there was no one around at all.

"This is where De Lorenzo lives?" asked Brooks.

Lefty nodded. "Casa de Lorenzo."

"Who lives here?" asked Layla.

"The dickhead we were talking about," said Dixie.

Layla nodded. "The one Daddy's gonna kill."

"Layla," said Lefty. "Let's not talk about Daddy killing people."

"Why not?"

"It's not nice."

"What's not nice?" asked Layla. "Killing people or talking about it?"

Lefty rolled his eyes. "Either one, Tator Tot."

"Then why do you do it?"

"Sometimes you gotta do things you don't wanna do to put food on the table."

Layla paused for a moment, considering this. "So you kill people for food?"

"Layla," interrupted Dixie. "Why don't we let your daddy think for a minute and figure out how he wants to do this."

Brooks turned to Lefty. "That's a good question. How do you wanna do this?"

"I honestly hadn't given it a whole lotta thought."

"You thought we'd just go rushing in there like the goddamn Wild Bunch?"

Lefty nodded. "Pretty much."

"Helluva plan you got, kid. I'm glad you got it all worked out."

"What's the Wild Bunch?" asked Layla.

Brooks turned to the little girl. "You ask a lot of questions, you know that?"

Layla smiled. "It's 'cause I'm curious."

"You are that, Tator Tot," said Lefty.

Dixie spoke up. "This sounds as poorly planned as anything I've ever seen."

Lefty looked back at her. "Thanks for your positive input."

"I just call it like I see it," Dixie said.

"How many guys you think are in there?" asked Brooks.

Lefty thought about it. "Probably as many as Liz Taylor had husbands."

Brooks leveled his stare at Lefty. "How many husbands did that bitch have?"

"Seven," said Dixie.

"But do we count it as seven or eight?" asked Lefty.

Dixie gave him a puzzled look. "Why would we count it as eight?"

"Because she married Richard Burton twice."

"He's still only one guy," said Dixie. "If he was two guys, we'd count him twice. But he was just one guy, so we count him as one."

"None of this is important," said Brooks. "I don't give a damn if Liz Taylor was married to forty-two guys, all named Jimmy, each with a ten-foot dick. That shit don't matter. What matters right now is this job. We need to discuss this before we go runnin' in there, gettin' our peckers shot off."

Lefty nodded.

"So there's probably about seven guys in there," said Brooks.

"Give or take," said Lefty.

"How many bullets we got?"

"I got a full magazine," said Lefty. "That's fifteen shots. Then I got another mag in my pocket."

"Christ, you could wipe out the whole hotel all by yourself," said Dixie.

"Why do you have so many bullets, Daddy?" asked Layla.

"Don't worry about it," said Lefty.

Brooks took no heed, speaking to this anyway. "He may need to shoot some of those SOBs more than once. Sometimes these bastards don't go softly into the night. Sometimes you gotta shoot a motherfucker three, maybe four times before they die."

Dixie looked at Layla. "Brooks, the little girl don't need to hear all that."

"Damn," said Brooks. "Lefty brings her along on a hit, lets her sing about all kinds of motherfuckers, but somehow I'm the bad guy."

Lefty looked at him, his eyes narrowing. "Is there something you wanna say about my parenting?"

Brooks returned his gaze defiantly. "I think I just said it."

Before Lefty could say another word, Dixie said, "The job, boys. Let's talk about the job."

"She's right," said Brooks.

"Okay, Dixie and Layla stay in the lobby," said Lefty. "They watch to see if anybody shows up unexpectedly or tries to run out."

Brooks looked at Dixie. "What are you gonna do if you see someone?"

"I'll do what I do," she said. "I'll kill 'em."

"What if a whole group of people come in?" asked Lefty.

"We shoulda got walkie-talkies," said Brooks.

Lefty exhaled, a judgmental expression on his face. "Walkie-talkies, Brooks? What do you think this is, *Scooby Doo*? Don't you think we might be noticed sneaking around the building with big-ass walkie-talkies?"

"They would definitely notice me sitting in the lobby if I was talking into a walkie-talkie," said Dixie. "That shit would be noticeable."

Layla said, "Can I have a walkie-talkie, Daddy?"

"How do we approach the penthouse?" asked Brooks.

"We knock on the door, tell 'em it's room service," said Lefty.

"That's kind of obvious, don't you think?" asked Dixie.

Lefty turned around and stared at her. "You got a better idea?"

Dixie shrugged. "No, but I doubt I'll have a worse one."

"You might," said Brooks. "Don't sell yourself short. You're capable of some super crappy ideas."

"Marrying you was the worst," said Dixie.

Lefty looked at Brooks. "How many rounds you got?"

Brooks held up his big Colt Python. "I just got this," he said. "It holds six bullets. Then I got more rounds in my pocket."

"Old school," said Lefty.

"Old school," agreed Brooks.

"I'd be afraid to use a piece of hardware like that," said Lefty. "It only holds six bullets at a time. What do you do when you're in a situation where there are that many guys total?"

"Shoot carefully."

"I'm serious."

"So am I," said Brooks. "I also got the shotgun in the trunk. If one don't get ya, the other one will."

"You're gonna carry both?"

Brooks nodded. "I am."

"You're a regular Johnny fuckin' Rambo."

"Nah, I'm just Brooks Barker."

"I suppose that's enough," said Lefty.

Brooks nodded. "I've put a lot of guys in the ground, and I'm still here. What does that tell you?"

Dixie looked up from staring at Layla reading her *Black Panther* comic. "Are we ready to do this or what?"

"I guess it's time," said Brooks.

They all started to climb out. Once they were out of the vehicle, Brooks made his way to the trunk. Lefty popped it open, and Brooks extracted the shotgun. Dixie came around and took out a .45, sticking it into her waistline. Lefty closed the trunk and they all turned towards the building.

Each adult had their handguns tucked away out of sight, but Brooks stood out carrying the shotgun at his side. They all strode through the entrance of the Belmont, the two men walking behind the females, the idea being maybe they would sort of block the desk clerk's view of the shotgun. When they walked in, Layla was explaining the difference between the Incredible Hulk and Abomination, but none of the adults were listening. They were scoping out the lobby. There was only one desk clerk, a pudgy little fat guy with a terrible comb-over. He barely glanced up from whatever he was looking at behind the counter.

The men and women separated, with Dixie and Layla making their way to chairs in the middle of the lobby. This way they could watch the smarmy little desk clerk to make sure he wasn't up to any fuckery. Lefty and Brooks went straight, heading for the elevator.

Dixie saw the clerk turn and watch Lefty and Brooks getting on the elevator. He paid Dixie and Layla no mind. He picked up the house phone and held it to his ear. He went to push a button, but Dixie took out her .45 and shot him in the throat. He grabbed wildly at his wound, blood streaming out between his fingers and onto his cheap suit. Dixie popped off a second shot, this one catching the pudgy bastard in his mouth. His head shot backwards, and he left a Rorschach blot on the wall behind him before toppling to the floor.

Dixie looked at Layla as she put away the .45. Layla's eyes were big as saucers and she was energized. "It was like Brooks said, you had to shoot him more than once to kill him."

Dixie nodded. "That happens sometimes. It ain't like the movies where everybody dies with just one shot."

"Why'd you shoot that guy?"

"He was gonna call upstairs and tell the bad guy that Brooks and your daddy were on their way. Then when they got there, Bruno and his guys would have killed them."

Layla's already big eyes got even bigger, and she opened her mouth, gasping. *"They were gonna kill Daddy?"*

"Oh yeah," said Dixie. "So it's like he said, it's okay to kill people who are gonna hurt the people you love."

"So you shot the fat man."

Dixie nodded. "I shot the fat fuck."

Layla raised her palm. "High five," she said. Dixie put her hand up and they slapped palms together. The little girl went back to reading her comic, and Dixie sat there in the empty lobby, watching for people to shoot.

. . .

Brooks and Lefty were riding in the elevator together, on their way to execute Bruno De Lorenzo. As they rode, Lefty asked, "How many men you figure you've killed?"

Brooks made a pained face. "Don't you know it's not polite to talk about how many people someone's killed? It's like sexual partners, it ain't right to talk about them. It's sort of disrespectful to the other person who's getting screwed or shot."

Lefty grinned. "Either way they're getting screwed."

This made Brooks grin too. "This is true."

"I'm sorry I asked. I didn't mean no harm."

"No offense taken, kid. The thing is, I've known guys who would brag about how many guys they killed all day long. But then there are other guys—"

"Guys like you."

Brooks nodded. "It's like a guy who returns from the war. It ain't nice to ask him how many Victor Charlies he killed out in the bush. And it ain't nice to talk about how many of these guinea scumbags a guy's racked up here in the states. Either way, a guy's just doing his duty, doing what he's ordered to do. He don't necessarily like taking those lives, but it's his job. It's what he does."

Lefty nodded. "You don't like killing people?"

"Depends," said Brooks. "I can't lie. There are times when it feels real good to kill someone, if it's someone you know deserves a bullet. Sometimes it feels good to be the one who does it. Like this guy Bruno De Lorenzo. If he did a fraction of the shit they say he did, then we'll be doing the world a favor."

"So in a way we're good guys, doing God's will."

"Could be," said Brooks. "Think about it. Everyone we kill is a criminal of some sort. None of them are good guys. They're all mobbed up, doing some kind of criminal shit."

Lefty said, "Like us?"

Brooks nodded. "I know, I know. Trust me, I see the fallacy of the theory, but I like to think it's at least somewhat okay because we kill more people than we are. Sure, you and I are basically bad guys, but in the end we kill hundreds of bad guys, most of 'em far worse than us."

"How do you know they're worse?"

"Good question," said Brooks. "Truth is I don't. I suppose it's a question of semantics. What do we really consider to be good, and what do we consider to be bad? I like to think we're lesser of evils."

"Lesser than who?"

"Someone like this bastard we're about to whack," said Brooks. "I feel pretty secure in the knowledge that he's way worse than either of us. Hell, he's way worse than both of us together."

Lefty nodded. "I'm sure you're right."

"I'm always right," said Brooks. "Don't you forget that, kid."

Lefty looked up, seeing that the elevator had arrived at the penthouse. "We're here," he said. At that moment the elevator doors slid open. The two men walked out, Lefty leading the way. They walked to the door of De Lorenzo's suite. Lefty shrugged. "Here goes nothing." He knocked, stepping out of the way so he couldn't be seen through the peephole. He saw it go black, indicating someone was peering out.

A moment later the door opened a crack, one of De Lorenzo's goons peering out past the chain-lock. "Who are you?" This time Lefty skipped the candy-gram routine and kicked in the door, snapping the chain and sending the guy reeling back. Lefty had his Glock up. He was about a millisecond away from shooting the guy when he realized the penthouse was empty. Disappointment set in at once. He aimed the gun down at the guy, on the floor now. "Where's everybody at?"

The guy sat up. "You're gonna have to kill me, because I ain't telling you shit."

Lefty squeezed the trigger, shooting him in the inner thigh. The guy reached for the wound, blood seeping everywhere. He was whimpering like a baby. "The next shot's gonna be your dick," promised Lefty. "Now where's everybody at?"

The man looked up at him with big, frightened eyes. "Don't shoot my dick, okay?"

Lefty smiled. "I'm not in the dick-shootin' business, but I could be at any moment. Tell me what I wanna know and maybe your dick lives to see another day."

Brooks raised his Colt, firing into the man's shoulder. The guy screamed again.

"He'll talk now," said Brooks.

"I had it taken care of," said Lefty, irritated.

"Sorry. I was just itching to shoot somebody."

Lefty nodded, looking back to the guy on the floor. "What's your name?"

"Dom," said the man.

"You ready to talk, Dom?"

"What do you wanna know?"

"Where's your boss?"

"Bruno?" Dom asked.

"How many bosses you got, shithead?"

"Well," said the guy. "Sometimes I work for Fat Pete, and sometimes..."

"Skip that," said Lefty. "Where's Bruno?"

"They're down at Bruno's restaurant."

"What's the place called?"

"Sabatelli's."

Lefty was about to ask Dom what street Sabatelli's was on, but Brooks shot the guy between the eyes before he could. Lefty looked at Brooks, who just shrugged. "Shit happens," he said.

TWELVE
BLOOD ALLEY

Lefty parked the Caddy down the street from Sabatelli's. It took some pleading with her, but Dixie agreed to stay in the car with Layla. "I came to kill some motherfuckers, not sit in the car and listen to jungle music," she said. Nevertheless, she stayed behind. Lefty and Brooks left Layla and Dixie in the Caddy with the AC blowing, Layla singing along to Teddy Pendergrass. As the professional killers strolled towards the restaurant, Lefty asked, "You think Layla will be safe with Dixie?"

"I do," said Brooks. "That woman is a lot of words a polite man don't say, but she can hold her own. And Layla's pretty tough too. She's a little adult. I pity the guy who tries to kidnap her. She might Ju Klemto the motherfucker to death."

As they approached the place, with its bright red awning hanging over the sidewalk and tables situated neatly out front, Brooks said, "Are we ready for this?"

Lefty said, "The question is, is Bruno De Lorenzo ready?"

The two men walked along the sidewalk with their guns

out. Lefty was carrying his Glock. Brooks had his big Colt Python in one hand and the shotgun in the other. When they came to the glass door, they entered, Lefty leading the way.

There was some kind of Italian instrumental music playing overhead. The place was empty except for the two tables of mobsters next to the left wall. The walls were as red as anything Lefty had ever seen, but they would soon be much redder. The place was lined with glass candle holders containing lit candles. The mood would have been perfect for a romantic date, but that's not what Lefty was here for. He had a date, but it was far from romantic.

"We're not open yet, nigger," said one of the men. Lefty recognized Bruno, having looked him up on the Internet. And he recognized the voice. "That's him," he said. The mobsters were all coming to life now as they figured out who and what their visitors were. All the Italians went for their guns at the same moment.

"*Kill these rat fucks!*" commanded Bruno, pointing at them.

Lefty and Brooks swung their weapons up simultaneously, moving in opposite directions. One of the mobsters fired first and someone turned over Bruno's table to provide them with protection. Within seconds there were shots flying around the room from all sides. One of the mobsters jumped to his feet and came charging at them, but Brooks caught him with a blast from the shotgun, sending his dead body flailing back, bouncing off one of the tables.

"*You motherfucker!*" yelled one of the men.

Lefty caught one of the mobsters in the eye with a clean shot, and the man went tumbling back.

As everyone fired back and forth and the windows broke and the restaurant was being shot to hell, a door to the kitchen opened and a burly paesan came rushing through it brandishing a butcher's knife. He was heading for Lefty, but only managed three steps out the door before Brooks blew him away.

A moment later another man emerged, this one firing a .38 and hitting Brooks in the arm. *"Motherfucker!"* Brooks screamed out, dropping the shotgun. Lefty fired two shots into the man's face, and the man was no more.

"Nice shootin', nigger!" yelled Bruno. *"That's what I'm gonna do to your kid!"*

Lefty heard the door opening behind him. Before he could turn, he heard Brooks' Colt ringing out, firing at the goombas entering. They fired into the restaurant, their bullets whizzing past Lefty's head. Lefty scanned the room for cover. Seeing the cashier's counter ahead, Lefty broke into a sprint. As he ran, a hail of bullets zipped past him from the group of mobsters on his left. He was several feet from the side of the counter when he dove, rolling to safety behind it. He popped up and turned his Glock on the goombas, returning fire. As he did, a bullet struck the metal register next to his head, causing the money tray to pop open.

It was at this moment Lefty saw Brooks take a second bullet in his stomach. Brooks went crashing forward, his Colt Python firing a round upward, obliterating a ceiling fan overhead. Brooks had now been shot in both the stomach and his arm, yet that didn't slow him down. He began to pull himself forward, sliding on the wooden floor, leaving a streak of blood behind. Before he could make any progress, one of the goombas who had entered through the front door moved towards him, shooting him in the head. Brooks flew forward, crashing into the floor. Brooks Barker was dead.

Lefty looked at his dead partner and newfound father figure, and suddenly everything went hazy. The man who killed Brooks turned towards Lefty. Before the mobster could get a shot off, Lefty fired a round of his own, catching the man in the throat. The mobster reached up for the instantly-bloody wound, flailing and flopping as he did.

"No!" screamed Bruno. "You killed Pino! You killed Pino, you moulignon fuck!"

Lefty turned towards the mobsters against the wall, firing at them, but his shot went wide. Another goomba popped up from behind the turned table and Lefty shot him in the chest, dropping him instantly. Bruno popped up now, firing off a round. Lefty took a shot at him, but missed, hitting the edge of the table.

One of the men flung something in Lefty's direction. It was coming directly at him. Out of sheer instinct, Lefty caught it, realizing immediately it was a pineapple hand grenade! Also out of instinct, Lefty hurled it back. The grenade exploded while it was still in mid-air. As a result, it only killed two of the mobsters instead of the whole lot of them it would have killed had it reached its destination.

Lefty grabbed one of the bottles of alcohol from behind the cash register. He saw that it was whiskey, and he turned, hurling it towards the wall beside the mobsters, catching them offguard. He fired a couple of shots at them before snatching a glass container holding a burning candle and hurling it against the wall. When the glass exploded, the whiskey caught fire and high flames erupted at once.

Bullets continued to fly. Lefty saw one of the mobsters squatting beside a table, trying to reload his Glock. Lefty let off a shot, hitting the guy in his arm. The man flopped around for a second, clutching at his wound. As he did, Lefty took a second shot, hitting him in the temple, killing him instantly. Another mobster bolted for cover. He fired at Lefty, but his shot missed. Lefty shot him in the head.

There were three mobsters remaining, standing beside the now-raging fire. Lefty fired, but didn't hit them. One of them returned fire in his direction. Bruno emerged, firing again. Lefty popped off a shot, striking Bruno in the side, and Bruno fell back out of sight.

Another of the mobsters moved away from the tables, into the center of the room. He popped off two shots in Lefty's direction, burying themselves in the counter. Lefty fired at him, hitting him in the cheek. There was now only the one mobster, crouched beside a table. Lefty came out from behind the counter and moved towards him. The mobster stood and fired. Lefty kept moving, shooting two rounds. One struck the mobster in the jaw, and the other in the ear.

In his peripheral vision, Lefty saw Bruno emerge from behind the table and take off towards the kitchen. Lefty spun and tried to fire, but the gun was out of bullets. Lefty stood there for a moment, ejecting his magazine and replacing it with another. When he was done, he ran towards the door, barreling through it with his gun up. Bruno was already out of sight, and Lefty knew he had to catch him if he was gonna get the money. He came to a corner on his left. He turned it, gun still out, and saw the back door standing open. Lefty rushed towards it, running into the alley. He looked to his left, seeing Bruno heading for an ambulance parked there, facing the opposite direction. Lefty fired a shot at Bruno, but missed him, striking the ambulance. The driver got out to see what was happening just as Bruno reached him. Bruno raised his pistol and shot the driver in the face. As the man fell to the pavement, Bruno hopped into the ambulance and shifted it into drive.

Lefty stopped and steadied his Glock. He fired twice at the left rear tire. At least one of the bullets hit their target, and the ambulance swerved into the brick wall. As Bruno struggled to regain control, Lefty fired a couple of shots, hitting the right rear tire. The ambulance swerved back and forth, scraping brick walls on both sides. Lefty was running again, hopping over the dead EMT. He wondered where the other EMT was—weren't there always two or three of them?—but kept moving. Suddenly the ambulance was slowing, almost to a stop. As Lefty reached it, he saw that a garbage truck was blocking the alley's entrance, trapping Bruno. Lefty ran around the left side of the stopped ambulance. He held his Glock up to the window in front of Bruno's face, motioning for him to get out. Bruno opened the door.

"Don't try anything stupid," Lefty said.

Bruno climbed out, still grinning.

"Drop your gun, Bruno."

Bruno dropped his pistol, which made a clanking sound as it struck the pavement. Still standing inside the open door, he turned to face Lefty. They were now eye to eye.

"Where's that little nigger girl?"

Lefty said nothing.

"How much money is my old man paying you to do this?" asked Bruno.

This surprised Lefty. "Your father is the one putting up the money?"

Bruno nodded, staring at him. "I don't know for sure, but I'm pretty sure it was that old cannoli-eating fuck."

"You've got a really fucked up family."

Bruno gave him a grin, still fully aware of his situation. "Tell me about it."

"Why would Don Antonio want his own son dead?"

Bruno shrugged. "I don't know. I guess I did a coupla things he didn't care for. What do you care, nigger?"

Lefty pressed the tip of his Glock against Bruno's right eye socket.

Bruno said. "I banged his *gumar*—his favorite one."

"That's it?"

"In the ass," said Bruno, adding, "And me and my boy Pino had a bukkake party with her. I filmed it and somehow the video ended up on the Internet." Bruno laughed. "And then he found out I was moving drugs for one of his rivals. He thought I was betraying him. I don't know, there were a few things like that. He also thinks I stole some money."

"So your dad put a hit on you."

Bruno nodded. "Apparently. How much is my contract anyway?"

"Two million."

Bruno looked impressed. "*Two million?* I knew the old man hated me, but damn. That's good, I guess."

"What do you mean?"

"It's a respectable figure. I'd be embarrassed if he was just offering a hundred thou for my head." He looked up at Lefty, completely serious. "Let's talk turkey, you and me."

"Gobble gobble."

Bruno smirked. Lefty didn't.

"Okay, you're a serious dude, I get it," said Bruno, nodding. "I got money. I got lots of money. I got more money than the Vatican got kiddie diddlers. He's offering you two million, I'll give you three. How about that?"

Lefty stared at him, unblinking, the Glock still pressed against his eye.

"Okay, okay," said Bruno, starting to panic. "There's no reason for this. Four million. I'll give you four million. What do you think? I'll give you four, you just walk away, and we pretend none of this happened."

"But it did," said Lefty.

"But did it?" asked Bruno. "Did it *really*?"

Lefty's finger tightened around the trigger. "Your guys killed my friend Brooks and you threatened my little girl. So yeah, it happened." Lefty lowered the Glock, firing a round into Bruno's knee cap. Bruno yelped, falling to the pavement. Now that Bruno was on his knees, Lefty slid his pistol into its holster. He put his hands around Bruno's head, his thumbs over his eyes. Lefty forced his thumbs forward, pushing them through Bruno's eyes. With Bruno's screams loud in his ears, Lefty pushed his thumbs into Bruno's head, feeling the wet eyeballs squish and pop beneath them. He removed his thumbs, looking down at what he'd done.

Bruno was on his knees, screaming, his hands up over his bloody eye sockets. He fell back into the open door of the ambulance. Lefty straddled him. He held Bruno's head down against the inside of the door with his right hand. With his left, he gripped the door. Mustering all the strength he could, Lefty slammed it hard against Bruno's head, smashing it. He did this repeatedly until Bruno's head crushed in and the goo from his eyeballs spurted back out. Lefty stood erect, staring down at the bloody pulp that was formerly Bruno's head.

Thinking it was over, Lefty started to turn, finding himself face to face with Dixie's .45.

"What are you doing here?" he asked, startled.

"What does it look like?"

"It looks like I'm getting screwed."

"Drop the gun, Lefty."

Lefty did as she instructed and dropped the Glock.

"Where's Layla?"

"I killed her."

Lefty was caught offguard and he felt his heart in his throat. *"You what?"*

Dixie laughed before saying, "The girl is okay, Lefty. I didn't hurt her. She's still listening to her shitty music in the car."

"Why are you doing this?"

"Isn't it obvious? I want the money."

"I was gonna give you half."

Dixie chuckled. "I know, but I want it all. Dixie doesn't do half."

"Was this always the plan? Were you and Brooks in on this together?"

"No," said Dixie. "It was always the plan for me, but Brooks had no clue. Truthfully, I was gonna kill him too, but somebody beat me to it."

Lefty stared at her in disbelief. "You were gonna kill Brooks?"

"I haven't cared about that sonofabitch since Bruce Jenner had balls."

"So you're gonna kill me?"

"Yeah," Dixie said dryly. "I'm gonna kill you."

Lefty shook his head in disgust. "What about Layla? What happens to her?"

Dixie sneered. "Why should I care about your goddamn kid?"

She repositioned the pistol, making a point to aim it right between his eyes.

"Say goodbye, dickhead," she said.

"Goodbye, dickhead."

At that moment a silenced shot struck Dixie in the side of her neck. Before Lefty could register this, there was a second shot, causing Dixie's brains to explode from her

175

head. She fell forward, her head striking the ambulance door. Lefty turned to see Orlando standing there with his pistol raised.

"You gonna shoot me now?" asked Lefty.

"Nah," said Orlando, grinning. "There aren't too many of us brothers in the biz. We gotta stick together. We're kindred spirits, you and I."

Orlando put out his fist. Lefty raised his hand, still holding the Glock, and bumped it.

Lefty nodded, catching his breath. "What do we do here?"

"We split the money down the middle. You were gonna split it with this bitch, now you can split it with me. Then we get out of Detroit."

Lefty nodded. "Sounds good, but why would you wanna team up with me?"

"Like I said, kindred spirits. Besides, I'm a man of honor. I could kill you now and take all the money, but I'm not that guy. Besides, I heard her say you had a daughter. Little girls need daddies." He paused before saying, "Let's go get our money."

"Wait a sec," said Lefty, fishing his cell phone from his pocket. He raised it, snapping a pic of Bruno's crushed head. "For proof that we killed him," he said. The two hitmen then turned and ran up the alley. As they did, a portly mustached EMT emerged from a door on their left. He was eating an oversized sub sandwich. Orlando raised his pistol at the EMT's head, and the man shrugged and went back inside. Lefty and Orlando continued running up the alley and around the building.

"Let's take my car," said Lefty.

"Sounds good," said Orlando. "Mine's fucked up."

"Have a fender bender, did ya?"

Orlando nodded. "Some asshole climbed on the hood and I had to get him off."

When they got back to the Caddy, Layla wasn't inside. "Christ," he said, looking around. "It's my little daughter. She's gone."

"What do you wanna do?"

Lefty looked down the street at Sabatelli's. "She musta gone looking for me. We gotta go back."

Orlando said. "I'll wait here."

Lefty turned and hustled back to the restaurant. He ran inside, stepping over the dead mobsters. The place was now filled with smoke, and there was fire raging all around. Lefty couldn't see. Fire and smoke was everywhere.

Was Layla here?

"Layla!" he screamed. *"Layla, are you here?"*

"Daddy!" came the frightened voice.

"Layla?"

"Daddy, help me! I'm trapped!"

Her voice came from within the bowels of the fire. Lefty was afraid of fire and never would have run into it under any other circumstance, but this was his little girl. This was Layla. Without hesitating, Lefty barreled into the fire. He squinted, trying to see, coughing on the smoke as he did.

"Layla!" he cried out.

"Daddy!"

He followed the voice. The fire was everywhere, and he could see nothing but glowing flames dancing madly around him. He continued his search, pressing on through the fire. Lefty and Layla continued to cry out for one another, back and forth, until Lefty located her. She was sitting on the floor, curled up, her hands squeezed tightly around her knees. She was crying. Lefty snatched her up, clutching her tightly to his chest. She whimpered as he did, saying nothing. He charged into the flames, running as quickly as he could. He could see the light of the entrance and windows ahead. He rushed towards it, trying to outrun the fire. He continued running, clutching Layla almost as tightly as she clutched him.

At last they emerged, frightened but unscathed. Lefty comforted her. "Everything's gonna be okay," he said. He held her tight, happy she was safe.

THIRTEEN
PLACES TO GO, PEOPLE TO KILL

LEFTY USHERED Layla into the Caddy, giving her a light push to encourage her to hurry. Orlando was on the passenger's side. Once they were all inside, Layla asked, "Where's Dixie and Brooks?"

"They're gone," said Lefty, pulling away from the curb. As he pulled into the street, several police cars sped past with their lights flashing and sirens blaring.

"Where'd they go?" asked Layla.

Orlando looked at Lefty, but Lefty ignored him.

"They had shit to do," said Lefty.

"Will we see them again?"

"I don't know," he said. "Maybe someday."

Lefty contemplated Brooks' and Dixie's deaths and how close he'd come to losing Layla. He looked back in the rearview. "How you feeling, Tator Tot?"

"I feel good," she said.

"How old is she?" asked Orlando.

"Seven," said Lefty.

"I had a daughter once. It was so long, long time ago."

. . .

A FEW MINUTES later they were in the gravel parking lot at Teaser's. There were a few cars scattered around, probably the same regulars Lefty had encountered the previous day. There were two black SUVs idling outside the entrance. Lefty looked at them as he parked out on the far edge of the lot.

"What do you think that's about?" asked Orlando.

"I guess we're gonna find out." Lefty turned and looked at Layla. "You stay here. And this time, no matter what happens, you keep your butt in the car and you duck down out of sight. You understand?"

Layla nodded.

"Layla," said Lefty, a sternness in his voice.

The little girl looked up.

"Are you sure you understand?"

She nodded.

"What are you gonna do?"

Layla said, "Keep my butt in the car."

"And?"

"Duck down out of sight."

Satisfied, Lefty and Orlando climbed out. When they did, they heard gunshots inside the club. The front door opened, and a goomba dressed in black came strolling out, looking around nonchalantly. Lefty and Orlando stood beside the Caddy, motionless, observing.

A moment later several mobsters emerged behind the guy. They were momentarily oblivious to Lefty and Orlando. One of the mobsters shielded his eyes from the sunlight as he stepped out. The men approached the SUVs, preparing to board them, when one of them noticed Lefty and Orlando. He turned and spoke to another guy, now pointing at them. Lefty couldn't hear what was being said, but he knew it wasn't good. Within seconds all of the mobsters were staring at them, raising their pistols.

"Oh goodie," said Lefty.

Orlando raised his Glock, the first man to open fire. His bullet struck one of the SUVs with a loud clang. Now the mobsters were firing back. *"Let's get away from the car so they don't hit Layla!"* said Lefty. They separated, still moving towards the strip club, doing a sort of half-run.

Bullets were flying all around. Lefty took a shot, hitting a particularly fat goomba right in the center of his belly. *"Ohhhh, I'm hit!"* cried the man. *"My belly, I'm hit!"*

None of the mobsters paid him any attention. They just went about their business, firing at Lefty and Orlando. One of the mobsters climbed into the driver's side of an SUV. A moment later, the SUV spun around, facing them. It came roaring towards them, attempting to run down Orlando. Orlando stood his ground, holding his gun steady. He popped off three shots in quick succession. The SUV swerved to its right, crashing into an ancient blue pickup. The SUV smoked a bit, but there was no fire or explosion.

The vehicle obstructed Lefty's view of the mobsters. One of them came running around it, but Orlando shot him, hitting him center mass. The goomba toppled face-first into the gravel. Lefty broke into a sprint again, going around the wreckage. As he did, another mobster came into view. He was staring up at him. The guy started to raise his pistol, but Lefty popped off two shots, striking him in the chest, and the man went down. Orlando fired a couple shots around the other side of the wrecked SUV, but Lefty couldn't see if he hit anything. Then Orlando disappeared around the other side of the wreckage. Not to be outdone, Lefty sprinted around the left side. When he popped out on the other side, he saw the last three mobsters. Two of them were ducked behind the still-intact second SUV, firing at Orlando. The other guy was just standing there dumbly, watching. He looked up at Lefty just in time to see him fire a round through his eye. It was the last thing the poor sonofabitch ever saw.

As the two remaining mobsters continued firing at Orlando from behind the SUV, he kept moving towards them. Now Lefty got into the act, striding towards them from the left. Both hitmen were firing at the goombas, their bullets striking the SUV. One of the mobsters ducked behind the vehicle, now out of sight. The other one kept firing at Orlando. Lefty shot the man in the side of his head. Just as he fell from sight, Orlando fired a shot that caused the SUV to explode. Lefty assumed the other mobster was dead from the explosion, but wasn't sure. As both he and Orlando moved in to investigate, the door to the strip club opened. Another mobster stood there, firing at them. Orlando turned and returned fire. His first shot struck the aluminum wall a foot to the left of the entrance, but his second shot hit the mobster square in the chest.

Lefty approached the fiery SUV. As he came around its side, he now saw the last mobster lying on the ground, reaching for his pistol. Lefty walked towards him, stepping on his hand, bones crushing beneath his foot. The mobster groaned, Lefty still on his hand. Orlando now came around the flaming SUV from the opposite side, his Glock aimed at the man. Orlando let off a shot, striking him in the head.

Lefty looked at Orlando. They nodded at one another, converging on the strip club. Orlando was the first one through the door. As they entered the dark club, the pulsing sound of techno music filled their ears. There were dead bodies sprawled out around the room. They made their way through the carnage, their Glocks at the ready ready.

Lefty went to Frankie Gio's office, where he found the greasy little bastard tied to a chair. He'd been beaten to a pulp and then shot in the forehead. It was gonna be difficult to get their money from him now. Lefty looked around the office, which had been ransacked. He looked down at a small safe, sitting there open with some papers hanging out. Lefty turned and walked out. He looked at Orlando, surveying the main room, and then entered into the Champagne Room. There he saw the stripper who'd given Frankie the lap dance lying there covered in blood. Lefty wondered if Candi was safe. He didn't know why he cared, but he did. He returned to the front just in time to see another mobster emerge from the shadows behind Orlando. The mobster raised his pistol to the back of Orlando's head and squeezed the trigger.

Click! Click!

"Dammit," said the mobster, holding up the pistol to examine it. By this time Orlando was turned towards him, confused.

"What the hell, man?" asked Orlando.

"I forgot to load the damn thing," the mobster said sheepishly.

Now Lefty was beside Orlando, both of them staring at the guy.

"Who do you work for?" asked Orlando.

The guy didn't even hesitate. He gave up the information immediately. "I work for Bruno De Lorenzo," he said nervously. "We were sent here to find out who put the hit on Bruno and to try and find the money if it was on the premises."

"Did you find it?" asked Orlando.

"No," said the man. "Bruno ordered us to kill Frankie when we were finished."

Lefty nodded. "I gathered that."

"From what?"

"From the fact that Frankie Gio's brains are all over the walls of his office."

"Ah," said the mobster, nodding.

"So who put the hit out on Bruno?" asked Orlando.

"Bruno's old man, Don Antonio."

"You must be a newbie," said Lefty.

"Yeah, I just started. My cousin Sal got me the job." He turned and pointed towards the entrance. "Sal was probably one of the guys you shot outside. You know, big fat guy?"

Lefty nodded. "Yeah, that was me. I shot him in that belly."

The mobster nodded, not seeming too broken up about it. "I never did like him much. He was always kind of a dick. One time when we were kids he poisoned my dog Benny, killed him dead as a Kennedy." The mobster paused for a moment before lighting up. "Hey," he said. "Before you guys take off, you gotta do me a solid."

Both hitmen stared at him in silence.

"Since I told you what you wanted to know, you gotta beat the shit out of me so it doesn't look like I helped you," said the mobster. "You know what I mean? I don't want Bruno pissed at me."

Lefty grinned. "I don't think Bruno's gonna be a problem."

"I can't take any chances," the mobster said, not comprehending. "I need you guys to really do a number on me, really rough me up, okay?"

Orlando shrugged and raised his Glock, firing a round into the guy's face. He turned and looked at Lefty, shrugging. "You think that classifies as roughed up?"

Lefty laughed. He couldn't help it, he really liked this Orlando, even if he had shot him in the shoulder.

"How we gonna get our money now?" asked Lefty.

"I guess we gotta go get it from Don Antonio."

Lefty nodded in agreement. "How do we get to him?"

"Hold on," said Orlando, heading into Frankie Gio's office. He searched both Frankie's body and desk for his cell phone, but couldn't find it. Then he spotted an old-school Rolodex on the desk, sandwiched between an Al Kaline bobble head and a framed photo of Frankie posing with Ron Jeremy. Orlando leafed through the Rolodex, finding an entry for Antonio De Lorenzo. He then returned to Lefty. "I got the man's number," he said, holding up the card. The two of them turned and stepped over dead strippers and customers, making their way back outside. There were no cops on the premises yet. Lefty looked out at the Caddy, still sitting there untouched. They walked out to the vehicle and climbed in.

Layla was eager to see them. "I'm glad you're back, Daddy!"

"I'm glad to see you, too, Tator Tot, but I need you to be quiet for a minute."

Orlando was on his phone, calling the number.

A man answered. "Yeah?"

"I need to talk to Don Antonio," said Orlando.

"Who's this?"

"I'm the guy who killed Bruno De Lorenzo."

There was a long pause. "Hold on," said the voice. There was an even longer pause now. Eventually the man came back and said, "I guess you want your money."

Orlando snickered. "I'm not in the business of killing for free."

To this the man said, "Riverside Marina at two o'clock.

Slip 222. It's a yacht named 'The Don Quixote.' Name's painted on the back."

"The Don Quixote?"

The man on the other end hung up.

"What now?" asked Lefty.

"We gotta meet 'em at Riverside Marina to get our money."

"When?"

Orlando looked at the dash clock. "Hour and a half."

"Daddy," said Layla.

"Yes?"

"I looked out the window and I saw you kill more people."

Lefty sighed. He didn't want her thinking killing was a normal activity, even if it was for him. "It's not a good thing to kill people."

"I know," said Layla. "But they were bad guys, right?"

Lefty sighed again, nodding. "They were bad."

Layla looked up at Orlando with big innocent eyes. "What's your name?"

"My name's Orlando," he said, grinning. "And I guess you're Tator Tot."

Layla frowned. "My name's not Tator Tot. Tator Tot would be a terrible name. Nobody is named Tator Tot!"

Orlando smiled. "What's your name then?"

"I'm Layla," she said. "Like the song by the white guy."

Orlando smiled, remembering what it was like to talk to a child. "It's nice to meet you, Layla."

"It's nice to meet you, too, Orlando," said Layla. "I like that name, 'Orlando'."

"Thank you. My mama and daddy gave it to me."

"I didn't know my mama," said Layla. "She died when I was born."

Orlando nodded. "I'm sorry to hear that."

Layla did a half-shrug. "Maybe she's up in the sky with Jesus."

Orlando nodded. "Maybe she is."

"Daddy doesn't believe in Jesus," said Layla.

"He doesn't?" asked Orlando. "How about you? Do you believe in Jesus?"

"Not really. I think he's made up like Santa Claus and the Easter Bunny. I think people pretend he's real to make themselves feel better. I think it makes them happy to believe there's a guy in the sky trying to help us."

"You don't believe there's a god who helps us?"

Layla shook her head. "Nope." She looked at Orlando solemnly. "Do you believe there's an Easter Bunny that helps us?"

Orlando laughed. "No," said Orlando, "I don't."

"Why not?"

"Because the Easter Bunny isn't real."

"Exactly," said Layla, staring down at her book.

Orlando looked at Lefty, who was looking in the rear-view, grinning.

"Smart kid you got," said Orlando.

"I hate to sound cocky and agree with you, but you're right."

"Orlando?" said Layla, looking at him.

Orlando turned to look at her. "Yes, Layla?"

"You said you had a little girl. What happened to her? Did she grow up?"

Orlando's expression changed immediately, going from happy to sad. He tried to hide it, but even Layla saw it.

"You look sad," she said. "What's wrong?"

"My little girl went to heaven," said Orlando.

"Maybe she's with mommy."

Orlando nodded. "I like to think so."

"How did she die?"

Lefty stopped her, looking in the mirror. "Layla, we don't ask things like that. It's not polite."

"No," said Orlando. "It's okay. She can ask." He looked at Layla. "She was going to school one day and she got hit by a car, right in front of the school."

Layla's eyes got big. "She did?"

Orlando nodded. "She did."

"What was your daughter's name?"

"Her name was Keisha."

"That's a pretty name."

"Thank you," he said. "I thought so, too."

"How old was she?"

"She was seven."

Layla lit up. "She was the same age as me!"

Orlando nodded, trying to hide his sadness.

Layla became serious again. "Do you miss her?"

"All the time," said Orlando. "I used to go visit her grave"

"Why don't you now?"

"I live a long way away now."

"Why did you move?"

"It's complicated."

Layla nodded. "I know what that means."

"What does that mean?"

"Daddy says 'it's complicated' when it's a grown-up thing he doesn't want to talk about."

Both Lefty, in the mirror, and Orlando, in the passenger's seat, laughed.

"You believe in God?" asked Layla.

Orlando paused, still looking at her. He considered his words. "I don't know," he said. "But I *want* to believe. I'm not sure any of it makes sense—people living in whales and that Noah's Ark stuff—but if there is a God, then that means my Keisha is alive."

Layla looked confused. "*Alive?*"

"Not alive, but up there in heaven."

Layla nodded. "With Mommy. And Jesus." She paused for a moment before adding, "And all those bad people you and my daddy killed."

Lefty rolled his eyes. He really hated hearing those words and was starting to regret telling Layla what he did. It went against every rule in the book, but Lefty wanted to be transparent. At least to a point. He wasn't gonna tell her he'd murdered her parents, but he also wasn't gonna lie about who he was.

Layla was sitting there contemplating all this. Finally, after a moment, she said, "I hope those bad guys aren't in heaven with Keisha and Mommy and Jesus."

"Why's that?" asked Orlando.

"They were mean," said Layla. "I don't want Keisha and Mommy and Jesus to have to shoot them in their heads because they're being bad. I don't think they would wanna do that."

Orlando looked at her. "Do you think Jesus would shoot them?"

Layla pondered this. "Yeah, if they were gonna hurt someone he loved, like maybe his daddy, then he would have to do whatever was necessary to protect them. It's like Brooks said, Jesus would have to blow their cunt asses away."

FOURTEEN
THE DON QUIXOTE

THEY ARRIVED at the marina a little bit early, allowing them time to figure out the layout and locate the boat. Both men agreed that Layla didn't need to be present for the meeting. Because Lefty didn't want Orlando to run off with the money, he wanted to be there. Because Orlando didn't want Lefty to abscond with the money, he agreed to watch Layla. There was a grassy hill next to a shop overlooking the marina. They found a picnic table there, and sat to wait until it was time for the meeting. The idea was that Orlando and Layla would sit atop this hill while Lefty went down and met with Don De Lorenzo or whatever goons he sent with the money.

"This reminds me of a song," observed Lefty.

Orlando looked at him. "What song is that?"

"Bitch Better Have My Money."

"I don't know that one," said Orlando. "Judging from the title, I'm gonna venture it's outside my wheelhouse."

Lefty grinned. "What kind of music do you listen to?"

"Classical," said Orlando.

"Damn, Orlando, how old are you? I didn't think anyone under the age of 400 listened to classical music."

Orlando smirked. "I could ask you the same."

"What does that mean?"

"I didn't think anyone over the age of 15 listened to rap music," quipped Orlando.

"Well, the song is almost 30 years old," said Lefty. "Back when hip-hop was good."

"I didn't know such a time ever existed," Orlando said.

Lefty ignored him.

Layla looked up, doe-eyed. "What's *classical music*?"

"Well," said Lefty, "it's this really boring, terrible music old people listen to."

Layla looked at him, unblinking. "Like Brooks?"

"No," said Lefty. "Old people like Orlando."

Layla scowled disapprovingly. "That's not nice, Daddy. Orlando's not old." Before Orlando could thank her, Layla added, "Not *that* old, anyway."

Orlando nodded, grinning.

"What are you gonna do with your share of the money?" asked Orlando.

"I'm gonna retire, hang up my guns."

Orlando nodded knowingly. "I tried that once."

"Didn't stick?"

"Nah, this shit is in my blood, I guess. I missed the life."

"So you came back?"

"I came back," said Orlando.

"How about you? What are you gonna do with the money?"

"I'll save it. It's not about the money for me. It's about the work."

"Well then," said Lefty, smiling, "if you don't want the

money, Layla and me would be glad to take it off your hands."

"Nah, I'm good. But thanks for the offer."

Orlando looked at his watch, seeing that it was close to two.

"That time?" asked Lefty.

Orlando nodded. "Yeah."

Lefty stood. He hunkered down over Layla, who was reading a *Guardians of the Galaxy* comic, and hugged her. "I love you, Tator Tot," he said. Layla didn't look up, but said, "I love you, too."

Lefty instinctively checked to make sure his silenced Glock was in its holster. Finding that it was, he straightened his jacket, bracing himself for the meeting. As he did, his shoulder began to throb. He winced. Seeing his expression, Orlando asked, "What's wrong?"

"It's my shoulder," said Lefty. "It hurts like hell." Lefty looked at Orlando. "Some bald-headed fucker shot me."

Orlando smiled. "I resemble that remark."

Lefty nodded solemnly. "You bet your ass you do."

Lefty turned and looked down at the boats docked on the water. "See you in a bit," he said, making his way down. As he did, Lefty considered this could be a setup. He didn't think it would be considering he was doing Don Antonio a favor, but there was no way to know. Where the Mafia had once been a calmer, more predictable place, events like Gotti whacking a boss (and Orlando later doing the same) and the introduction of drug sales and RICO, the organization had changed. The business had become the Wild West. These days people would rather shoot a guy than look at him, so a mob associate—especially a black one—had to watch his ass at all times.

But maybe this was legit. Maybe they would hand over

the money, Lefty could divide it up with Orlando, and everyone could go about their merry way.

Maybe.

Lefty reached the edge of the dock, stepping onto it. As he made his way along the walkway, he paid close attention to the slip numbers, watching them as they got closer and closer to 222, where the Don Quixote was. Finally he came to the slip, and there, as promised, was the yacht. Lefty knew nothing about boats, having never been around them, so he was unsure about this. There was no one in sight. He figured whoever he was supposed to meet was inside the yacht, but he didn't know if he should just yell for them or board the thing and knock.

"Hello?"

No one responded, and he was forced to step onto the boat. He hopped on, momentarily struggling to find his footing. He regained his composure and knocked on the closed door. A moment later the door opened and a skinny Italian with slicked back hair answered. The goomba wasn't wearing a suit like the usual mob guy, but rather a red Hawaiian shirt.

"Who are you?" asked the man.

"I'm the guy who killed Bruno."

"How'd you do it?"

"I crushed his head in."

"Interesting." The goomba stepped out of the way, allowing Lefty to enter the cabin. Lefty didn't feel comfortable, but he did what was expected and stepped inside. Once the door was closed, the goomba said, "Can I offer you a drink?"

"No, I'm good. I'm just here for the money."

"Right," said the man. "Of course."

He walked over to a table, sitting on a couch behind it.

There was a leather briefcase on the table. The man reached for it, turning it so the combination locks were facing him.

He man clicked the locks, opening the case.

"Here's your money," he said.

Lefty stood there, tensed up, just in case the goomba tried anything.

The man smiled, coming up from the case with a .45 aimed at Lefty. Before gun could clear the lid, Lefty slid his Glock out as effortlessly as Clint Eastwood in a Spaghetti Western. The Glock came to life and bullet holes simultaneously appeared in both the briefcase and the goomba. The man's face twisted into a gruesome display, and he fired haphazardly, firing a round into the wall.

Lefty knew there was no money in the case—why would there be?—but he moved forward and checked anyway. Just as he thought, there was no money there. The briefcase had been empty save for the gun.

Lefty turned and walked out of the boat's quarters. When he stepped outside, he heard the sniper's bullet strike the wall to his right. He looked over and saw the hole. He looked around frantically, but had no idea where the shooter was. The guy had a rifle, could be anywhere. Lefty turned and re-entered the cabin, a second shot smashing into the door.

What could he do? What were his options? There really were none he could think of beyond waiting inside. But what would he wait for? Would another gunman come rushing inside, or would the sniper simply fire holes into the hull, sinking the *Don Quixote* with him inside?

Lefty waited, but heard no more gunshots. Finally, he grew tired of waiting and stepped outside. He stood there for a moment, staring up at the hill overlooking the water, searching for the sniper. He saw nothing. The guy could be anywhere.

Suddenly another shot ripped into the exterior of the cabin, right beside Lefty's head. It took a moment for Lefty to register it. When he did, he dove back inside the cabin, waiting for someone to come to kill him.

The mobsters did not disappoint. After Lefty had waited awhile, the flimsy door came smashing in, revealing a mobster wielding a gun. However, Lefty was sitting inside the door waiting. Before the mobster could get clear of the door, Lefty put a bullet in his head. The guy fell out of the way, his body blocking the entrance. Lefty sat there a moment, his gun trained on the door, one hundred percent sure there were more gunmen. A minute later, a second mobster poked his head around the corner, firing a gun into the cabin. Lefty fired at his face, splintering the door frame beside him. The man was no longer visible, hiding out on the deck.

The man reached around the doorway, his pistol aimed into the cabin. He fired wildly, shooting nowhere near Lefty. Lefty, however, siezed the opportunity. *"Unnnngggghhhh!"* he cried, feigning being hit. Seconds later the gunman came in, catching a bullet in the eye for his trouble.

Lefty exited the cabin, looking towards the shore, searching for the sniper.

ORLANDO WAS SITTING at the picnic table, talking with Layla about her favorite Prince songs. Since Orlando didn't listen to pop music, he had no idea Prince had once been in a band called 94 East. But somehow seven-year-old Layla knew all about it.

"You're a smart kid."

Layla nodded. "I know."

Orlando smiled, surprised by the lack of humility.

"Do people tell you that a lot?"

"What?" asked Layla.

"That you're smart."

"Oh, yeah. Everybody says that."

"Do you think it's true?"

Layla looked at him, trying to determine whether or not he was insinuating she was stupid. "Well, yeah, of course I do," she said. "I'm the smartest girl in my whole class. There are other smart kids, like Devon, who's almost as smart as me. But she believes in aliens. You know, from outer space."

Orlando stared at her. "And you don't?"

"Of course not. Do you?"

Before Orlando could answer, he heard a sound coming from the bushes to their left. He squinted, trying to make out what was happening. When he did, he saw a man crouched there, aiming a sniper rifle at the docked boats. Orlando looked in that direction, trying to see Lefty, but found he could not. But Orlando knew Lefty was the target.

"Hold on," said Orlando to Layla.

He stood up, crouching down a bit, moving briskly up the hill at an angle towards the gunman. Orlando had his Glock up, ready to shoot if push came to shove. Eventually he would shoot him no matter what, but he didn't wanna do it from this distance. He continued moving towards the bushes. As he did, he heard the zip and saw the rifle rock. Orlando burst into a sprint now, charging towards the sniper. He must have made a noise, because the sniper sat up, half out the bushes. The gunman fumbled around, probably reaching for a handgun. Orlando leveled the Glock, firing a bullet into his temple. The man fell back, his brains painting the bushes behind.

Orlando wished he had a way to tell Lefty the sniper was dead, but he didn't have his phone number. He couldn't leave Layla alone, and he sure couldn't take her down on the dock. So for now Orlando would just have to sit and wait for his return.

He sat down, scanning the area for more would-be assailants. As he did, Layla explained the genesis of Prince's first solo album. They sat talking for almost an hour before Lefty made his way back.

As Lefty approached, Orlando asked, "Didn't go well, huh?"

"Not particularly."

"I'm guessing it was a set-up?"

"There was a guinea on the boat, waiting to kill me. After I shot him, a couple more goons rushed me. Then, on top of all that, there was a sniper up here taking pot shots. I never did see where he was."

Orlando turned and pointed towards the bushes. "He's over there."

Lefty looked over, raising his gun.

"No worries," said Orlando. "He's deader than Abe Vigoda."

Lefty approached Layla, hugging her from behind. "I missed you, Tator Tot."

"I missed you, too, Daddy."

"What did you guys do?"

"Well," said Layla. "I told Orlando all about Prince, and Orlando killed another bad guy." She looked at Lefty. "How about you, Daddy? Did you kill some bad guys?"

"I don't wanna talk about it."

Layla nodded. "I know what that means. That means 'yes.'"

Lefty grinned. "How do you know so much?"

"Because I'm smart, Daddy."

"You take after your daddy," said Lefty.

Layla made a face.

"What?" he asked. "You don't agree?"

"You're pretty smart," said Layla. "But not as smart as me." Realizing she may have hurt his feelings, she added, "But you're still smart, Daddy. You're not *too* dumb."

Lefty rolled his eyes.

"So now what?" asked Orlando.

Lefty sighed. "I guess we gotta go after Don Antonio. Get our revenge, and get our money."

FIFTEEN
GOING TO WAR

They were driving down Rosa Parks Boulevard in Lefty's Caddy. Orlando took out his cell phone and called his friend Moses. Moses was an old Mafia associate, a "friend of ours" they called him. He fenced stolen goods and operated a sports book with permission from the organization. Moses knew everyone and everything involved with the crime world in Detroit. You couldn't boost a car or snatch a chain without Moses knowing about it ten minutes before it happened.

"Hey Moses, this is Orlando."

"Orlando, my man," answered Moses. "How's it goin', youngblood?"

"I'm in your neck of the woods. I need an address."

"No problem. Who you lookin' for?"

"Don Antonio," said Orlando.

"Sounds like you got big fish to fry."

"Moby Dick."

"The great white whale."

"Man owes me money. I come to collect."

"You got a pen and paper?"

"No," said Orlando. "What I got is something better."

"Which is?"

"A photographic memory."

"You want the man's home or his office?"

"Where does he spend most of his time?"

"Man spends almost all his time at home these days."

"Then home it is."

"Don Antonio lives in Palmer Woods. You know Palmer Woods?"

Orlando asked, "That Tiger Woods' brother?"

The old man laughed. "Nah, it's a white bread neighborhood lined with great big nigger-free houses filled with uppity crackers. Palmer Woods is up there north of Seven Mile Road. Don Antonio lives there on Woodward Avenue in a big white house with red trim. Gaudy as hell, that red trim. Looks like Liberace threw up all over the house. You can't miss it. And it's got a great big clock out front, hanging next to the door. Can you believe that? Who the hell puts a great big ugly-ass clock on the front of their mansion?"

"A man who wants to know what time it is?"

"That man wouldn't know what time it was if Father Time kicked him in his ass," quipped Moses. "So, you gonna shoot the man?"

"I can't say."

Moses laughed. "Same old Orlando."

"A gentleman doesn't kill and tell."

"Sure you right."

"Thanks for the info."

"No problem," said Moses. "And keep your black ass out of trouble."

"You know me better than that."

Orlando ended the call. He looked at a map of Detroit on his phone, trying to figure out how to get to Don Antonio's house. Once he and Lefty determined the best route, they discussed the situation.

"What's the play here?" asked Lefty.

"We gotta get our money. That's the only play there is."

"Yeah, but do you think he's gonna have that much money on hand inside his house?"

"Probably not," said Orlando.

"Then what?"

"Then we take his fat ass to the bank and get the money."

Lefty looked at him. "How you know he's fat? You seen him?"

"Nah, but these mob bosses are all fat."

Lefty nodded, recognizing the truth in this.

"What do we do after we get the money?" asked Lefty. "Do we kill him?"

"Is there a choice?"

Lefty grimaced. "I guess not. But the organization will have us killed." He looked at Layla in the rear-view. "They could hurt her. Or worse."

Orlando looked at Lefty, maintaining a serious expression. "You want out?"

Lefty considered it. He knew the answer he should give, which was 'yes,' but he also knew the answer he would give, which was 'no.' "Like the song says, it's too late to turn back now."

Orlando nodded. "Ain't that the truth?"

"It's a hell of a life, this life of ours."

"But the pay is good, and what else are we gonna do?" observed Orlando. "We gonna work nine-to-five jobs wearing suits and ties and sitting inside a goddamn cubicle staring at a screen?"

"Not me," said Lefty. "But I heard you used to be a professor."

"Once upon a time."

"Why'd you give it up?"

"Because I had to kill a mob boss and his minions."

"*Deja vu.*"

"All over again."

MOSES WAS RIGHT—THE house was unmistakable with its giant clock and tacky red trim, sitting there nestled among a slew of bland, all-white, lookalike mansions. Lefty drove past the place so they could give it a look-see. There was a single goon standing by the door, right next to the clock. There were sure to be more goombas inside. Lefty parked the Caddy a full block down the street, planning to walk down to Don Antonio's just as he had when he'd saved Layla.

"I'm gonna have to leave you here for a few minutes, Tator Tot," Lefty said.

Layla frowned. "You said this was gonna be a fun trip. This isn't fun at all. You said we were gonna go to an amusement park, but we haven't. It seems like most of the time I'm just sitting in the car waiting for you to go kill bad guys."

Lefty and Orlando exchanged looks.

"Again, we really shouldn't talk about Daddy killing people," said Lefty.

Layla sounded irritated. "I know, Daddy."

"If you said it to the wrong person, Daddy could go to jail for a long time."

Layla nodded. "Probably for a year."

"No," said Lefty. "Probably forever. So no more, okay?"

Layla nodded. "It's boring sitting here in the car. Is this gonna take a long time?"

"We'll hurry," said Orlando. "I promise. Then we'll be right back."

"Tell you what, Tator Tot," said Lefty. "I'll make it up to you. Tomorrow, when this is all over, Daddy will take you someplace fun."

Layla looked up, her face brightening. "Like where?"

Lefty didn't know. "We'll just have to see what we can find. I don't know what they have that's fun in Michigan. I don't know this place."

"An amusement park?" asked Layla.

"We'll just have to see what we can find."

"I wanna go to an amusement park."

"We'll find one soon," said Lefty. "I promise. If we don't find one tomorrow, we'll find one soon. I'll make sure when this is over we'll do some fun things. When this is all over, you'll have Daddy all to yourself. I promise."

Layla nodded, her expression indicating she didn't believe this.

"What kind of music do you want me to play while I'm gone?"

"Well," said Layla, "I was talking about Prince earlier, so how about that? I wanna listen to *Purple Rain*."

"The album or the song?"

"The whole thing."

"*Purple Rain* it is," said Lefty. He dug out the CD and slid it into the player. A moment later, Prince came on. "Dearly beloved..." and so on. Lefty and Orlando stepped out of the car. "I love you, Tator Tot," said Lefty. "I love you, too, Daddy," said Layla, looking down at her comic. The two men walked to the trunk, opened it, and reloaded their weapons. After all, a guy needed plenty of bullets when going to war with a mob boss.

Lefty and Orlando strode towards the house, their pistols by their sides, looking like something out of a movie. When they got to the yard, they turned up the empty driveway, walking towards the house. Before they reached the top of the drive, the goomba on the porch started moving towards them.

"Who the hell are you guys?" he asked. It was then he saw their guns, and he ducked behind a pillar, raising his own. The goomba fired first, missing Orlando by a country mile.

Lefty's fired, his bullet striking the pillar. The mobster came around again, his gun up. Before he could fire, Orlando shot at him, striking his gun. The goomba cried out in pain, dropping his pistol. Now unarmed, he tried to duck back behind the pillar, but there was nowhere to go.

Lefty came up on him first, maneuvering around the pillar with his Glock aimed at the guy. The gomba put his hands up in front of his face, trying to shield himself.

"No, no," he begged.

"Where's Don Antonio?" asked Orlando.

"Please don't shoot me."

"Just tell us where the Don is."

"He's upstairs," said the mobster. "Are you guys gonna shoot me?"

Lefty's pistol answered the question, providing a response the mobster probably didn't like. Not that he knew, not for more than a millisecond at best, before his blood contributed to the red trim on the house.

Lefty didn't miss a step when he shot the man, continuing to move towards the front door. Orlando was at his side, slightly behind. Both men had their guns up, ready for action.

Even though Lefty reached the door first, Orlando stepped forward and rang the doorbell. They could hear the god-awful long-bonging chime, just as gaudy as the house itself. A moment later the door opened and a skinny goomba with a five o'clock shadow appeared. He looked around.

"Where's Vic?" he asked.

Orlando pointed at the dead guy lying on the ground.

"Vic didn't make it," said Lefty.

The guy looked over, saw the body, and suddenly came to life. He went for his gun, but Lefty stuck his own up under the man's chin, squeezing the trigger.

Orlando stepped forward, leading the way through the door. He stepped inside, narrowly being missed by a flying bullet. Orlando raised his pistol, still moving, and fired at the blur of motion to his left. Despite not having a clear view of the gunman, Orlando's bullet struck paydirt, hitting his kneecap. The guy fell over, screaming in agony. Before Lefty or Orlando could react, the fallen mobster was sitting up, firing again. Orlando fired a second volley at him, this one burying itself in his eye.

"*What the fuck?!*" came a male voice from another room. Before Lefty and Orlando could register what was happening, the guy with the voice came charging from the hallway, firing. Lefty maneuvered to his left, moving away from Orlando.

The man fired at Lefty, shattering a window behind him. Orlando fired, striking him in the stomach. The guy made a loud moaning sound, doubling over. The top of his head was exposed, and that's where Lefty shot him.

"Nice shootin', Tex," said Orlando.

"Thanks," said Lefty, surveying the room. He looked up at the top of the stairs in the center of the room. Just as he did, another mobster emerged up there, taking a shot at them. Lefty moved further to his left, crouching behind a baby grand piano. As he did this, Orlando took cover behind a table, only partially concealing his body. The mobster fired down again, his bullet striking the piano and making an onimous *"dunnn"* sound. Lefty popped off another shot, his bullet striking the railing. The guy started to take another shot, but Orlando fired at him, missing, causing him to retreat. The mobster ducked back into the room from which he'd come, and neither hitman could see him. They both kept their eyes glued to that door as they gradually made their way up.

Orlando and Lefty were midway up the stairs when the mobster emerged again, popping off a couple of shots but completely missing them. Both Orlando and Lefty's Glocks fired simultaneously, both of them hitting the man. One of them hit him in the forehead, and the other at center mass. The two hitmen made their way up towards Don Antonio's bedroom. They were at the top of the stairs when another goomba emerged below, firing up.

Lefty looked at Orlando. "How many of these fuckers are there?"

"Too many."

Lefty and Orlando held their ground, firing down on the mobster now crouched behind the piano. They let him fire unopposed for a moment. Finally, the guy rose from behind the piano with his gun raised. As he did, Orlando fired, shooting him in the chest.

Lefty and Orlando were in the upstairs walkway, crouched behind the railing. Lefty looked at his partner. "You think there's more of them?"

"I hope not. All this killing is wearing me out."

They both stood, Orlando leading the way towards the master bedroom. When Orlando opened the door, Frank Sinatra came blaring out. Orlando surveyed the room, but saw no one. There was a closed door, presumably a bathroom, at the far end of the room. That's where the music was coming from. That was where Don Antonio was.

Orlando walked stealthily, opening the door. When it was open, they saw a hairy, heavyset, balding old man, probably seventy, standing naked in a hot tub, facing them with a cigar in his mouth. This was obviously Don Antonio. There was a naked young brunette standing beside him, washing his chest with a sponge. Don Antonio and the girl looked up at them, somehow shocked despite all the gunshots. Sinatra's loud crooning must have muffled the sounds of the bloodbath.

The old man's body stiffened, and the young woman moved away from him. "What the hell do you guys want?" growled Don Antonio.

"We're here for our money," said Lefty.

"What money?"

"The money for killing your fuckhead son," said Orlando.

Don Antonio looked at them for a beat, his half-smoked cigar dangling from his lip. Suddenly a second naked woman, this one blonde, emerged from beneath the water. She was facing Don Antonio, unaware of Lefty and Orlando. She held up a wash rag and announced, "Your balls and asshole are clean now."

Don Antonio looked past her, staring at the two men in his bathroom. "How dare you come in here like this!" The ball-and-ass-cleaning woman now looked around at them, seeing them for the first time.

"Should we have scheduled a meeting?" asked Orlando.

"That way you coulda set us up again," added Lefty.

Don Antonio stared at Orlando. "I know who you are. You're that no-good jig who killed a boss."

"And I know who you are," countered Orlando. "You're the no-good wop who owes us two million dollars."

"You killed a boss," repeated Don Antonio.

"Do you want me to kill another one?"

Don Antonio's eyes grew bigger and his face turned red. "How big are your balls that you come into my home—my sanctuary—and threaten me?"

Orlando smirked. "My balls are pretty big."

Lefty chuckled.

Before Don Antonio could respond, a side door burst open and another naked girl appeared, carrying an AK-47. *"Alright, you sonsofbitches!"* she screamed. She and Lefty looked at one another, their eyes locking.

"Candi," said Lefty.

Candi lowered the weapon. "Lefty... I didn't know it was you."

There was an unmistakable chemistry between them. Lefty liked Candi way more than he should have liked a stripper, and he wondered if she felt the same way.

"You work two jobs?" he asked.

"Not really," said Candi. "Don Antonio owns Teaser's, so I just do whatever he needs me to do."

Lefty started to respond, but the reunion was broken up when a naked Don Antonio, now out of the tub, came charging at him. The old man shoved him back against the sink. As Lefty's back struck the edge of the counter, he felt a sharp pain. He looked up at the old man, surprised. Orlando raised his pistol towards Don Antonio, but Lefty motioned for him to lower it. "Nah, I got this," said Lefty. "Let me deal with this guinea bastard."

He lunged towards the naked man, connecting with a solid uppercut. It was a punch that would have knocked many a man out, but Don Antonio was a tough old bastard. He just stood there, naked and dripping, shaking it off. He put his fists up like an old-time brawler. He wasn't dancing around like those guys, but he was circling Lefty slowly.

"You think you can barge in here and attack me?!" asked Don Antonio.

"I did, didn't I?"

Don Antonio lunged at him again, punching Lefty in the shoulder where he'd been shot. Lefty staggered back in pain, his back and shoulder hurting. He caught himself and regained his composure.

"What's your end game?" Lefty asked. "You gonna beat us both up, naked, with your fists, and then walk away unscathed?"

Don Antonio didn't speak. Instead he moved forward, swinging wildly at Lefty's head. As the old man swung past him, Lefty connected with another uppercut, this time to the chin. This one seemed to ring Don Antonio's bell. He staggered back, shaking his head. The old man then forced himself back into the moment, raising his fists once again.

Lefty rushed him, shoving Don Antonio into the hot tub. The old man fell in with a splash, landing next to the naked women. As Lefty climbed over the side, going into the water after him, the women started scrambling out. Within seconds Lefty was on Don Antonio, his hands gripped around his neck, holding him underwater. Lefty rocked back and forth, shoving his head deeper under water.

"*Lefty!*" interrupted Orlando. "*You can't kill him! We need to get our money!*"

Lefty was staring down at the old man's ever-reddening face beneath the water, his eyes bulging. Lefty considered Orlando's words, finally pulling Don Antonio's head up out of the water. Don Antonio hung limply in his arms, all his fight now gone.

SIXTEEN

WHEN DOVES CRY

A FEW MINUTES later Don Antonio was conscious again, getting dressed in the bedroom. The two body-cleansing women had been allowed to leave after Orlando had convinced them not to tell what they'd seen. Candi was still there, now fully dressed in a tight shirt and skimpy shorts that exposed half her ass.

"When you guys leave, can I catch a ride?" she asked.

"Where to?" asked Lefty.

"I gotta work at the club."

Lefty and Orlando turned to one another, exchanging a look. Candi saw this and asked, "What? What was that look?"

Lefty said, "Teaser's is gone."

"What do you mean?" asked Candi.

"Yeah," said Don Antonio, sitting there pulling his socks on. "What do you mean 'Teaser's is gone'?"

"They're all dead," said Lefty.

Candi's eyes got big. "All of who? Who's dead?"

Orlando said, "Everyone. The strippers, the bouncer, the DJ, the customers, Frankie Gio. Everyone."

Don Antonio became angry. *"You black fuckers shot up my club?"*

"No," said Lefty. "Bruno sent his men over there to find out who put the contract out."

"Everyone's dead?" asked Candi, starting to cry.

"Did Bruno find out who put the contract out?" asked Don Antonio.

"He hadn't found out yet when I talked to him," said Lefty. "But he had a pretty good idea. He told me he thought it was you."

This caused Don Antonio to smile proudly. "Good. I want him to know."

Candi was standing there, heaving and crying. Lefty put his arms around her, comforting her.

"It's okay," said Lefty. They pulled back a moment, staring into one another's eyes. "It's gonna be okay," he repeated. Candi leaned in and kissed him.

Don Antonio paid them no mind. "So Bruno had Frankie murdered," he said. "Figures. He never did have any respect for rules or traditions. Bruno didn't have respect for anything, except pussy and money. That's it. That's the kind of crap that got his ass in this predicament in the first place."

"Well," Orlando said dryly, "he's not in a predicament now."

Don Antonio looked up at him, grinning. "So you guys killed him, huh?"

"Deader than Lincoln at the play."

"That makes me happy. It really does. It gives me a raging hard on. It warms the cockles of my heart to know that ungrateful little piece of shit is gonna be worm food. I never liked him, even a little bit. Never, ever. Even when he was a little kid, he was a goddamn heathen. He was the worst. Even his mother hated the little prick." Don Antonio looked at Orlando. "Can you imagine that, a mother hating her own kid?"

"Yeah," said Orlando. "Your son sucked."

Don Antonio slipped on his shoes.

Lefty stepped away from Candi. He turned to Don Antonio and said, "Now we're all gonna go to the bank and get that money together."

Don Antonio looked up at him as he tied his shoe. "You sure you don't wanna continue your romance with this little piece of ass? I've had her, and lemme tell you, she's good."

Candi stepped towards Don Antonio and spit in his face. Don Antonio licked the spit from his lips, unfazed. He looked at Lefty. "What makes you think I'm gonna give you that money anyway?"

Orlando raised his Glock at Don Antonio's face. "You'll give us that money if you wanna live another day."

"The question is, why didn't you just give us the money in the first place?" asked Lefty. "We did a job for you. You clearly owed us the money, fair and square. Why pull that shit on the boat?"

Don Antonio shrugged. "It wasn't personal, kid. I know that sounds like bullshit, but it's the truth. It's seldom personal in out business." He paused for a minute, thinking. "Well, with Bruno it was personal. That was a thousand percent personal." He caught himself getting off topic. "But the thing is, it wasn't personal with you at all. Two million dollars is a lot of money. Two million dollars will always be a lot of money. And, well, hitmen are expendable."

Lefty made a face. "You mean black hitmen."

"No, that's not what I meant. When it comes to two million dollars, everyone is expendable. Literally everyone. This wasn't about race or any of that. This was only about one color, and that color was green. Money talks, bullshit runs the marathon. It's as simple as that, son."

"After we get our money, say we let you live," said Lefty.

"Yeah?"

"Would you still kill us?"

The old man smiled a comforting grandfatherly smile. "It was just business, kid, and I owe you the money. Besides, you did me a solid here by killing that little cunt-monkey Bruno. Really, you did everyone a favor. The whole world really."

"So you wouldn't kill us?" asked Orlando, studying him.

"Well, you did kill a bunch of my men..."

"Correction, we killed *all* your men," said Lefty.

Don Antonio looked displeased. Nevertheless he said, "I deserve that. What's a man of honor who's got no honor? If I continue down this path, I'm no better than Bruno. I don't want that. I don't wanna be Bruno. When I die and hopefully go to heaven, I don't wanna meet St. Peter with that shit on my conscience. Lord knows I've done enough bad shit in my life, I don't need to add to it now."

"So you won't have us killed?" Orlando asked.

"You got my word," said Don Antonio. "I won't have you killed. But there will be some qualifiers."

Lefty looked at him. "Such as?"

"You gotta leave Detroit, and you can't ever come back. Not ever. Seriously. Twenty years pass by, even when I'm dead and moldering in the dirt, nothing left but a decayed corpse, you still can't come back. People will know. Trust me, people are gonna know. Bad people. If you so much as show your face to go to a Tigers game, someone'll be there at the concession stand to pop a cap in your ass. So it is written, so it shall be done. I know I owe you the money, but you killed my guys. I can't let that slide without some sort of repercussions."

"That's fine," said Lefty. "Who the hell wants to be in Detroit?"

Orlando nodded, looking down at Don Antonio. "Can I ask you a question?"

"Ask away."

"Tell me this: losing all your men, was that worth two million dollars?"

Don Antonio grinned. "Most of them were shit anyway, and like I said, everyone is expendable when it comes to two million dollars. Everyone. I mean, you're talking to a man who killed his own son, so why should I care about these clowns?"

Don Antonio was saying the right things, but Lefty wondered if he would keep his promise. There was no way to know for sure. Lefty didn't know what Orlando's thoughts were, but he himself was still 50/50 in regards to letting the man live. At this point it could still go either way.

Orlando looked at Don Antonio. "You ready to go, old man?"

Don Antonio nodded. "Sure, let's go."

Candi looked up at Lefty, her big brown eyes sweet and innocent. "Can I still get that ride?"

"Where to?" asked Lefty.

"Wherever you're going."

"You mean now?"

"I mean forever," she said.

TEN MINUTES later they were all in the car with Lefty and Layla in the front, Orlando, Don Antonio, and Candi all smooshed together into the back. Orlando was sitting there holding his gun on his lap, the barrel facing Don Antonio. Prince was still playing, but it was turned way down so it was barely audible. Despite its low volume, Layla was still bobbing her head to the music.

"I don't keep my money in a bank," Don Antonio said.

"Where do you keep it?" asked Lefty. "Under a mattress?"

"I got a guy who holds it for me. His name is Parker, but we just call him the Banker. He takes care of my finances and keeps all my money."

Orlando asked, "What's to stop somebody from robbing him?"

Don Antonio looked at Orlando, a serious look on his face. "The fear of God is what. Everybody knows you don't steal from Don Antonio. You do that, you end up in a fuckin' hole quicker than you can say 'please don't kill me.'"

"Please don't kill me," Candi deadpanned.

"You laugh now, and that's okay," said Don Antonio, "but if you stole my money it'd be a different story. Your pretty little ass wouldn't be sittin' here making jokes right now."

"So this guy the Banker," said Lefty.

"What about him?" asked Don Antonio.

"Where do we find him?"

"He's got an office in a warehouse down on the pier."

Orlando asked, "How do we know this isn't another set-up?"

"You don't," said Don Antonio. "No way you can. But think about it, how would I have known we'd be doing this? I certainly haven't called him. You know that because you've been with me the whole time."

"So how do we get the money?" asked Lefty.

"We go to the warehouse. The banker sees me, he'll give us the money. Simple as that."

Hearing "When Doves Cry" playing beneath the adults' conversation, Layla piped up. "Can we turn this up, Daddy? Pretty please. It's my favorite."

Lefty shrugged. "I gotta turn it up," he said. "You can't argue with 'When Doves Cry.'"

Lefty turned up the volume and music filled the car, Prince singing about animals striking curious poses.

"This isn't music," said Don Antonio. "This is just noise. The stuff these kids listen to today is garbage."

Candi asked, "How the fuck old are you? The kids who listened to this song are all middle-aged now."

"The album was released in 1984," explained Layla. "The song was number one in the United States."

This amazed the adults. "Wow," said Candi. "That's impressive. How old are you, kid?"

"I'm seven and five-eighths," said Layla.

"You sure know a lot about music for such a little girl," said Don Antonio.

Layla beamed. "My daddy taught me all about it. But just good music, no country."

Candi laughed. "You don't like country?"

"Oh no," said Layla, deathly serious. "Daddy says the only thing worse than country music is the redneck assholes who listen to it. He says they sleep with their sisters, whatever that means." She looked back at Don Antonio. "Are you one of those assholes?"

He smiled. "I'm a different kind of asshole."

Layla looked at him with doe-eyed innocence. "What kind of asshole are you?"

"I'm just an old guinea who likes listening to guys like

217

Frank Sinatra and Tony Bennett," said Don Antonio. "Do you know about those guys?"

"Nope," said Layla. "Like I said, I only know about good music."

Everyone in the car chuckled at this. Layla was oblivious to the laughter as she listened to Prince.

WHEN THEY ARRIVED in front of a nondescript door at a nondescript warehouse, the three men got out of the Caddy. Lefty, Orlando, and Don Antonio walked towards the place. Don Antonio knocked hard. A moment later, a heavyset man with a bad comb-over answered. He looked at the two black men, alarmed at first, and then his gaze fell on his boss.

"Oh," said the man. "I didn't know it was you, Don Antonio."

Don Antonio raised his fist to the man, exposing his gold ring, and the man kissed it. "This is the Banker," said Don Antonio.

Lefty gave a half-hearted nod to the man, and they all entered the warehouse. The Banker led everyone through the dark building to his office. The office was a dank, dimly-lit room with concrete walls. It was smokey, smoke filling the room from a half-smoked cigarette sitting in an ashtray that was overflowing with spent butts. There was a calendar with half-naked models on it and a clock showing the incorrect time hanging on the wall. There was a cheap low-rent metal desk in the center of the room, covered in crinkled papers and stains from where the man had sat his coffee mug over the years.

The Banker sat down behind the desk. There were two metal folding chairs in front of it. Don Antonio took one and Orlando took the other, leaving Lefty standing there chair-less. The banker looked at Don Antonio. "I see you've got different guys working for you now."

Don Antonio shrugged. "Nah, these are just some guys I owe some money to."

The banker's brow furrowed, and his eyes looked over the two black men, silently trying to determine their motives.

"Nothing bad," assured Don Antonio. "We got an understanding."

"What kind of understanding?"

"The kind you don't need to know about."

The banker sat back, blinking, visibly hurt by his not being included.

"I see," he said. "So what can I do for you?"

"I need some money."

"When?"

"Right now," said Don Antonio.

The Banker looked at the two hitmen again, still suspicious.

"How much?"

"Two million."

It was clear from the look on the Banker's face that the amount startled him. *"Two million?"* he asked. "That's a lot of money."

"It ain't chump change," said Don Antonio.

"And you need it now?"

"I need it now."

The Banker was clearly unsure what his move here was. He bit his lower lip, considering the Don's request. Finally, he stood up and walked to the door. "I'll be right back."

The Banker left and the three men waited in silence.

About a minute later, the Banker walked back through the door with a .38 aimed at Orlando.

"No," said the Don. "When I said there was nothing funny going on, I meant it. Now I'm gonna ask you one more time—and only one more time—go get me my money before I break your goddamn neck."

This did the trick. The Banker looked hurt again, lowering both his gaze and the gun. "Alright," he said weakly, turning away. He then disappeared again. He didn't return for several minutes. When he did, he was carrying a black duffel bag. He sat it in the doorway.

"This is all of it?" asked Don Antonio.

"No," said the Banker. "This is half. I'll have to go and bag up the other half. It'll take me a few more minutes."

The Banker disappeared from sight again, presumably to get the rest of the money. Don Antonio sat there in the aluminum chair. He motioned towards the bag. "You wanna look in it, make sure I'm not screwing you?"

"No, we're good," said Lefty.

"Why's that?" asked Don Antonio.

"Because you don't wanna die today," said Orlando.

Lefty moved forward, picking up the bag. He looked at Orlando. "Keep an eye on him. I'll put this in the trunk and be right back."

Orlando nodded, looking at Don Antonio.

As Lefty walked out of the room, he heard Orlando say, "Thanks for stopping the Banker. That could have been a bad deal for everybody."

"Don't worry about it," said the Don. "I gave you my word and I intend to keep it."

Lefty walked out of the dark warehouse and into the bright sun. He walked to the car, which was only a few feet away. He opened the trunk, sitting the bag inside it. Neither

Candi nor Layla paid him any mind. He closed the trunk and walked back into the warehouse. He returned to the office. The Banker had not yet returned, so Lefty took a seat behind the desk.

"Did you take a photo of Bruno's body?" asked Don Antonio.

"We did," said Lefty.

"Can I see it?"

Lefty pulled out his phone and brought the image up onscreen, handing it over. Don Antonio stared at the photo in silence for a moment before erupting into hearty laughter. "I guess you could call that a crushing defeat!" he said. He handed the phone back to Lefty, saying, "I like that. You guys did good work. Bruno looks better than he ever did."

"You swear you're not gonna come after us if we let you go?" asked Orlando.

"How many times and ways can I say it?" asked Don Antonio. "I'm a man of my word. I know I fucked up by trying to have you whacked out there at the pier, and I'm genuinely sorry for that. There's nothing I can do about that now."

"Well," said Lefty.

"What?" asked the Don.

"You could throw in a couple hundred thousand extra. You know, just for the trouble and all."

The old man grinned. "Yeah? And you could suck my dick, but I'm assuming you're not going to, just as you might assume I'm not giving you a dime more than the two million I owe you."

Lefty nodded. "Can't blame a guy for trying."

"No, you can't," said the Don. "You don't get anything in life if you don't ask for it."

Just as Don Antonio was finishing his sentiment, the

221

Banker filled the doorway, carrying a second black bag. "Here's the rest of it," he said, sitting it down.

"There you go," said Don Antonio. "Now I would advise you to take the money and get out of here while I'm still feeling charitable."

"You're not gonna wish us safe travels?" asked Orlando, smiling.

"Safe travels, motherfuckers," said Don Antonio, laughing a big belly laugh. "Now get the fuck outta here."

Orlando picked up the duffel bag. "Nice doing business with you," he said, heading for the exit. No one said a word. Lefty followed Orlando. When Orlando opened the door, the bright sunlight pouring in, he saw Layla sitting on the concrete Indian-style, scratching the ground with a rock. The Cadillac was gone.

Both Orlando and Lefty looked around for a moment, the realization of what had occurred now coming to them.

Lefty knew what had happened, but he asked, "Where's Candi, Layla?"

The little girl looked up at them nonchalantly. "She said she had to go. But she told me to tell you she was sorry."

Lefty and Orlando stood there for a moment, staring at one another in disbelief. Lefty momentarily worried that Orlando might believe he and Candi were in on the whole thing together, but that didn't seem to be the case.

"Well," said Orlando, "half a million isn't really all that bad."

Lefty looked off in the distance where Candi had obviously driven. "You sure you don't wanna track her down? We could do that."

"I'm tired. I think I've killed enough people for today."

Lefty looked down at the little girl sitting on the concrete. "Get up, Layla," he said. "It's time to go home."

She stood up and the three of them started walking down the street away from the warehouse.

"Daddy," said Layla.

"Yes, Tator Tot?"

"Can we go to an amusement park now?"

Lefty sighed. Orlando chuckled at this.

"What?" asked Layla.

"Sure, we'll go to an amusement park," said Lefty.

"Right now?"

"Not right now, but we'll go."

"When?" asked the little girl.

"As soon as we can get the fuck out of Detroit," said Lefty.

Orlando agreed. "Good riddance."

THE END

Orlando and Lefty will return.

Dear reader,

We hope you enjoyed reading *Layla's Score*. Please take a moment to leave a review in Amazon, even if it's a short one. Your opinion is important to us.

Discover more books by Andy Rausch at https://www.nextchapter.pub/authors/andy-rausch

Want to know when one of our books is free or discounted for Kindle? Join the newsletter at http://eepurl.com/bqqB3H

Best regards,
Andy Rausch and the Next Chapter Team

ABOUT THE AUTHOR

ANDY RAUSCH is the author of nearly forty published books. His fiction includes *Riding Shotgun and Other American Cruelties*, *Bloody Sheets,* and *The Suicide Game*. His nonfiction includes *The Films of Martin Scorsese and Robert De Niro, The Cinematic Misadventures of Ed Wood*, and *My Best Friend's Birthday: The Making of a Quentin Tarantino Film*. He is also a screenwriter, graphic novelist, and journalist. His work has appeared in a variety of publications including *Shock Cinema*, both *Screem* and *Scream*, *Diabolique* (where he is also an editor), *Cemetery Dance*, *Scary Monsters*, *Cinema Retro*, and many others. He resides in Parsons, Kansas, and became a heart transplant recipient in 2018.

You might also like:

Chloe – Lost Girl by Dan Laughley

To read the first chapter for free go to:
https://www.nextchapter.pub/books/chloe-lost-girl